THE ENGAGEMENT GAME
49TH FLOOR SERIES

JENNY HOLIDAY

Entangled Publishing, LLC
2614 South Timberline Road
Suite 109
Fort Collins, CO 80525
Visit our website at www.entangledpublishing.com.

Indulgence is an imprint of Entangled Publishing, LLC.

Edited by Tracy Montoya
Cover design by Heather Howland
Cover art from iStock

Manufactured in the United States of America

First Edition September 2015

For the real-life Jo.

Chapter One

Rosie glanced down at her buzzing phone.

Josephine Withers

Her initial reaction — *what the hell?!* — was followed by panic. Something had to be wrong for Jo to call. Texting was one thing — it had been grandfathered into their friendship — but *talking*? With their *voices*?

Rosie had been exchanging paper letters with her best friend Jo since Jo's family moved away when both girls were twelve. Since then, they had religiously exchanged a letter per week. A *letter*. Written by hand. On *paper*. As they grew up and long-distance telephone calls became less of a big deal, Rosie stubbornly clung to the idea of a weekly handwritten letter — you didn't just abandon a tradition that had been going strong for fifteen years — though they also emailed and texted pretty much daily.

But calling? Jo knew Rosie hated the phone. The last

time they'd spoken on the phone was two years ago when Rosie's dad died. Heck, they saw each other in person for visits more than they called each other.

"Hello?" Rosie was breathless. The way her stomach fluttered, it might as well have been tonight's Match.com date. Rosie had high hopes that the guy, who was presenting extremely well via text, would turn out to be "the one."

"I think you made a mistake," said Jo, "with your last letter?"

Rosie wanted to say, "Huh?" but Jo was talking so fast she couldn't squeeze it in.

"I thought if I called you might still have time to fix it don't yell at me I know you hate talking on the phone I'm going to read it and then hang up and it will be like this never happened."

"Uh, okay?" was all she could think to say in response to that epic run-on sentence.

"Dear Mr. Rosemann—"

Rosemann. As in Marcus Rosemann. As in millionaire Marcus Rosemann, to whom she had just sent a thank-you letter for his sizeable donation to EcoHabitat Toronto, the nonprofit for which Rosie worked.

"Thank you for your generous gift in support of..."

Oh, no. No, no, no, no.

Rosie dropped the phone as adrenaline surged through her limbs, making them shake. When she picked it up, Jo was still talking.

"It's donors like you, whose regular commitments we have come to rely on, who will truly help us realize our goal: a city in which humans and animals—and their habitats— can coexist peacefully."

Sending the donor thank-you letter to Jo, and the gossipy, nattering note intended for her best friend to Marcus Rosemann wasn't just a *mistake*, to use Jo's term, it was a fireable offense. As the charity's fundraising manager, she was the *last* person who should be making such a careless error. "Shit, shit, shitballs!"

"Sweetie, calm down. You do everything at that place. You're allowed to make one mistake," Jo said.

"Triple shitballs!"

"Who's lined up as tonight's Mr. Thursday Night?"

Every Thursday night, Rosie went on a date with a guy from one of the many dating sites she used, and Jo had adopted Rosie's practice of referring to each of her suitors as "Mr. Thursday Night." Rosie appreciated that Jo was trying to change the subject, to return her attention to something mundane and routine, but she had to fix this letter mix-up. She had to fix it *now*. "Jo. I love you, but I gotta go."

Dear Jo,

I'm a day late writing this. I thought about forging the date, but I knew you would KNOW somehow, so I'm just going to come clean. I'm a day late. So shoot me. I was busy this weekend.

With what, you might ask? Was I busy with the latest Mr. Thursday Night, one Mr. Mark Larson, second grade teacher?

Yes, but not in the way you might think.

But, oh, my dashed hopes! Wah! He taught seven-year-olds! He was kind and gentle! He did not have (as far as I could tell) a secret wife/child/family/cocaine habit/sex addiction/storage locker full of vintage typewriters. (He did, however, have an unfortunately untidy—bordering on gross—beard in this whole "I look like a logger but I've never even been camping" way that seems to be all the thing. But a girl can't have everything. A girl becomes suspicious, in fact, when presented with everything. So I was good with the beard. Mostly.)

The problem was not the beard. It was that in addition to teaching seven-year-olds, he had the alcohol tolerance of one. Which would not have been a problem if he had owned up to this, and we could have adjusted our consumption accordingly. But three tequila shots later, he was barfing in my lap. On that new dress I texted you a pic of.

So when I got home, all I could do was make a cup of tea and take a shower. I was not in letter-writing mode. And here I thought I might make a Mr. Thursday Night into a Mr. Friday Morning. No. A thousand times no. Maybe I should start listening to my mother.

But! Once more unto the breach, dear friend! If I want to find a boyfriend, I've got to get back onto the horse, right? I have a couple options for this Thursday and am leaning toward TallDoctor83, with whom I've exchanged a few messages. Who doesn't want a tall doctor, right? If I had pink eye, he wouldn't even have to stoop to examine me. (Har! Ladies and gentlemen, I'm here all week.)

And what about you? The hubs is still adoring you, no doubt? (As he should!) And Toby? Is he conjugating French verbs yet? Or still only just rolling over? The last pic you sent was so ridiculously cute it made my teeth hurt, and if I didn't love you so much, I would hate you.

BFFs!
xoRosie.

What the? Marcus turned the letter over, as if the back of the pink floral stationery would yield some clue as to the prank someone was obviously playing on him. Nothing. He grabbed the crisp ivory envelope it had come in. Yes, all was in order here. The return address was EcoHabitat Toronto, the ecosystem conservation charity he'd been financially supporting since his mother died nearly a year ago.

But instead of the usual canned thank-you letter from whichever wizened gray-haired society matron was currently chair of the board, he had this...pink thing.

There was a tap at the door, two soft raps he recognized as his assistant. "What is it?" he asked when she popped her head in, murmuring apologies. Carla never came in when he'd blocked off work time.

"I'm so sorry," she said, looking close to tears, which was highly unusual for the take-no-prisoners admin assistant.

"What's happened?"

"Your father's on the phone. I know you said no calls from him, but I—"

He knew immediately what she wasn't saying. The thought that his father had been bullying his capable and loyal assistant shoved him right into that familiar groove, the one lined with four decades of resentment.

"Put him through."

"I tried telling him—"

"Put him through."

Carla nodded and backed out of the room. A moment later, his phone buzzed. He picked it up. "What?"

"Are you bringing a date Saturday?"

Here we go. "I told the aunts I don't know yet."

"It's forty-eight hours away, Marcus."

"And why have you taken such an interest all of a sudden? The Fall Ball was Mom's thing." *And we all know how much you cared about her.*

"All eyes will be on our family," his father lectured. "*Especially* this year, with your mother…gone."

Marcus snapped a pencil in half.

"Don't you think it's time you settled down?" his father went on.

Marcus heard everything his father didn't say. *Come back to the firm. Get married to someone I approve of, and have two-point-three kids. Conform.*

It would be easy enough to find a date. Any of the women he saw casually would be delighted to accompany him to the social event of the season. "I'll bring someone," he snapped, and hung up. But the moment he did so, he regretted his easy capitulation. He scrolled through the contact list on his phone. All of these women were...perfectly suitable. Most of them were wealthy and ran in the same circles as his family. All had impeccable manners and social instincts. His father would be pleased to see any of them on his arm on Saturday.

He returned his attention to the absurd letter from EcoHabitat Toronto, staring at it as if it were a life preserver keeping him tethered to his sanity.

The ink was green, for God's sake.

It wasn't like he objectively gave a shit about EcoHabitat. But his mother had. So it irritated the hell out of him that this "xoRosie" person was sloppy enough to mix up her letters, which was what he assumed had happened. Marcus had no tolerance for carelessness. It signified a lack of discipline. Wasted potential.

He had half a mind to march over to EcoHabitat's office and give xoRosie a piece of his mind. Or maybe xoRosie's boss. The only thing stopping him was the thought that that was something his father would do.

He pulled up the charity's website, which was a complete mess—not at all intuitive, difficult to navigate. Perhaps instead of money, he should offer his company's services pro bono to straighten it out. A professional ad agency could do a lot for EcoHabitat.

Eventually, he managed to land on a page labeled, "The team."

Ah—there she was. Rose Verma, fundraising manager. He cocked his head, squinting at the overexposed headshot next to her bio. In addition to a better website, EcoHabitat also needed a better photographer. But even so, it was easy to tell that she was a beauty. Long black hair, a killer smile. She looked a little like that TV star that Lauren, his executive creative director, was obsessed with. Mindy Something.

So she was sloppy, undisciplined, *and* beautiful.

He picked up the shards of the pencil his father had caused him to destroy, and an absurd idea took hold. An evil-genius idea.

Why the hell not?

Yes, the train wreck known as Rose Verma would do quite nicely.

"All right, if that doesn't dazzle TallDoctor83, he should change his handle to Tall*Blind*Doctor83," Hailey declared, capping the lipstick she'd just applied to Rosie's lips. EcoHabitat's receptionist moonlighted as a makeup artist, and she always insisted on doing Rosie's face for her Thursday night dates. Sometimes the looks were a little extreme—with her goth style, Hailey herself looked like a cross between a MAC saleswoman and the Corpse Bride—but the result of her makeup applications was always better than anything Rosie would have been able to achieve on her own.

Since Rosie was meeting TallDoctor for drinks at the upscale Thompson Hotel, she'd asked Hailey to give her a classic smoky eye. Her personal makeup artist had added a matte magenta lip. Rosie eyed her reflection in the hand mirror Hailey held. She looked *good*. Sometimes, when she saw herself like this, dressed up and made up, she thought back to her lonely, miserable middle school years. After Jo had moved away, she'd had plenty of alone time to fantasize about what life would be like when she escaped the white-bread suburb her family lived in, where she stuck out like a sore thumb. Back then, she'd imagined herself an independent career woman living in the big city, getting ready to go on a date. And look at her now. "I would never have known to try a color like that," she said of the lipstick. "How do you *do* that?"

Hailey winked as she packed up her cosmetics bag. "It's a gift."

Rosie gave herself a final once-over. If only she weren't so damn tall. "Well, if he's into Indian giantesses, he will definitely be dazzled."

"Who *isn't* into Indian giantesses?" Hailey deadpanned.

"Um, the last Mr. Thursday Night, and the one before that, and the one before that." So maybe she *wasn't* so far from the gangly, awkward teenager who didn't fit in. Because although she went on plenty of first dates these days, second dates—not so much.

"I don't know if you can really say that about the last one. If he hadn't barfed on you, who knows where things would have gone?"

It was true. To be fair, Rosie was—outwardly, anyway— not the awkward ugly duckling anymore. She rejected men more than they rejected her. She was on Mission: Boyfriend, but she wasn't going to settle for just anyone. She was looking for a life partner, after all. A father to her future children.

She was looking for love. So she had high hopes for TallDoctor.

She always did.

"You going home first? Want to walk to the subway with me?" Hailey asked.

She shook her head. "Nope. I'm not boarding any critters at the moment, so there's no need to make a pit stop. I have tons to do here, anyway. Mr. Carroll wants—"

"Ah, ah, ah!" Hailey showed Rosie her palm. Then she looked at her watch. "It is 6:27. I've been off the clock for fifty-seven minutes, and I won't tolerate any talk about Mr. Carroll. The fact that Mr. Carroll is in charge around here and not you is a crime against humanity."

Rosie grinned. EcoHabitat's executive director was universally disliked by his staff. He was basically an incompetent, mansplaining ass, so it was easy to see why. Rosie sometimes felt bad for him, though. It must be difficult to go through life so completely clueless yet with responsibility for important things like, oh, say, the well-being of entire ecosystems. But Hailey, who was young and still undisappointed by life, had no tolerance for human failings of any kind. Still, Rosie appreciated the show of loyalty. She pretty much did everything that was in her job description and half of what was in her boss's. In her more ambitious moments, she fantasized about deposing him somehow. Mr. Carroll's ineptitude got in the way of so many of their projects.

"Hit the lights, will you?" Rosie said as her friend waved good-bye. "I'll leave out the back when I'm ready."

The lights in the hallway flicked off one by one, and Rosie heard the *thunk* of the heavy door at the top of the stairwell. Her office was located on the third floor of the converted Victorian that housed EcoHabitat. It had been left to them by a wealthy benefactor three years ago. Though it had allowed them to move out of the cramped, expensive space they had been renting in a nearby office building, the place was still a little rough around the edges. They'd been plowing what they used to pay in rent into renovations, but having started from the ground level and worked their way up, they hadn't made it to the third floor yet.

In truth, Rosie kind of liked the creaky old bedroom that functioned as her office. The slanting attic walls still papered in a Laura-Ashley-style pattern from the 1980s and the uneven wood floors had a lot more charm than her cubicle at the old place.

"Rose Verma?"

She shrieked and reared back, which caused her chair to roll backward toward the door, and, given the slope of the floor, she just kept rolling. There was nothing to grab. She glided ingloriously to a stop at the feet of the visitor.

The ridiculously hot visitor.

He had blue eyes with laugh lines around them and thick, premature salt-and-pepper hair. With his gray, exquisitely tailored suit, he looked like a corporate lawyer, or a banker.

"I'm Marcus Rosemann."

Or, you know, the head of an ad agency and one of EcoHabitat's most important donors.

Another shriek. The reaction was involuntary. She rolled back to her desk and literally banged her head against it a few times. Why not? It wasn't possible to humiliate herself with this man any more than she already had. Head still resting on the desk, not caring that her speech was muffled by her arms, she said, "*Please* tell me you got the second letter." The letter she'd FedExed, explaining the mishap and assuring him that the lapse had nothing whatsoever to do with the general standards of professionalism and decorum observed by the organization.

"Mr. Rosemann, so nice to meet you," he said, his voice oddly devoid of inflection. She lifted her head from its hiding place and narrowed her eyes. Was he mocking her? "Your mother was such a devoted advocate of this fine organization. I'm delighted to finally meet her son."

She sat all the way up. "How did you get in here?"

"How can I help you, Mr. Rosemann?" He held up the letter. She'd known he had it, but, oh God, seeing it there, the flowery stationery clasped in his big hands—it was too embarrassing. "Especially given the recent mix-up with our correspondence. How will I make it up to you?"

Geez. Was he really so mean that he would come here and throw an innocent mistake back in her face? "Because the receptionist left before you got here, so I'm not really sure how you got in." Her instincts told her that she, if not her pride, was perfectly safe, but the rational part of her brain was starting to realize that she was alone in the building with this angry stranger who was holding in his hands not only her letter, but the fate of her continued employment at EcoHabitat. Because all he would have to do is call Mr. Carroll, and that would be it for Rose Verma, fundraising manager.

"If by *receptionist*, you are referring to the heavily pierced woman with the fauxhawk, she let me in on her way out. She told me that even though it was obvious I was lying about 'the 1983 thing,' at least I was actually tall."

"Oh, she thinks you're TallDoctor83!" Yeah, Marcus Rosemann looked like he had a few too many years on him to be born in 1983. If she had to guess, she'd peg him as late thirties. But he was certainly tall—she could see why Hailey had made the mistake. She had a feeling if she stood up, he'd still have a good few inches on her. That hardly ever happened.

She stood. Yup. She still had to tilt her head back a little to give him a look.

He took a step forward and waved the letter back and forth. "Do you want me to examine you for pink eye?"

In another context, the question could have been a joke. Rose had a lot of experience recognizing jerks, though, and the deadpan delivery and the slight curling of his lip made it clear that Marcus wasn't kidding. And that he was a jerk.

But he was an epically handsome jerk—wasn't that always the way? She looked closer at him. His eyes weren't straight up blue. They had a tinge of gray. And his five o'clock shadow, like his hair, was streaked with silver. Dear God, she had a weakness for scruff on a man.

He looked right back, one eyebrow raised.

Still a jerk, though. These rich philanthropists often were—they were the grown-up versions of captain of the football team, or the head cheerleader.

It was just that rich philanthropists weren't usually so… delicious. Her cheeks started to heat. So she capitulated, ceding the weird staring contest she seemed to be having with Marcus Rosemann.

Marcus Rosemann! What was the matter with her? The fate of her job hung in the balance here, and that was more important than any amount of personal mortification and/or attraction she might be experiencing.

So she took a step back—and a deep breath. "Mr. Rosemann, so nice to meet you. Your mother was such a devoted advocate of this fine organization. I'm delighted to finally meet her son." He lifted his eyebrows when he realized she was parroting his earlier words exactly. She kept going. "How can I help you, Mr. Rosemann? Especially given the recent mix-up with our correspondence? How will I make it up to you?"

"You'll come with me to the Fall Ball Saturday night."

Whaaaat? The sense that she was maybe getting this slow-motion train wreck under control evaporated. "Excuse me?"

"It's a charity ball my family organizes," he said, as if this explained everything.

"I know what it is." EcoHabitat had been the beneficiary one year. They'd raked in more than their usual annual fundraising take on that one night.

"It's going to benefit breast cancer this year. My mother died of it ten months ago."

She knew that too, but the way he stated it so matter-of-factly took her aback. Rebecca Rosemann had been a big supporter of EcoHabitat and had served on its board until she became too sick to continue. "I was so sorry to hear about her passing. We all were."

"So you'll come." It wasn't a question.

"You just met me!" Was this guy on crack?

He held up the letter. "And yet I feel I know you so well."

"I *am* sorry about that." She made a face. "Mortified, actually."

He stepped inside the small office, filling it with his commanding presence, let the letter flutter down to her desk, and looked between it and her, a question in his eyes.

"You just met me," she said again, as if saying it enough times would make him see how ridiculous he was being.

"Is that idiot Tony Carroll still in charge around here? He and my mother go way back. I'm sure he'd be very interested to learn how careful his employees are with correspondence to EcoHabitat's major donors."

Her mouth fell open. "Are you *blackmailing* me?"

The crinkles around his eyes deepened as he pressed his lips together. It looked like he was trying not to smile. "I believe I am."

As she stood there with her bright pink mouth hanging open, Marcus almost started laughing. But that would have ruined the menacing vibe he was going for. Rose Verma was the perfect date for the Fall Ball—the perfectly imperfect date to rile his father—and he had to have her. He pulled out his phone. "Give me your contact info. I'll pick you up at six on Saturday."

As he watched her eyes narrow, he fancied for a moment that he could see the gears turning in her head. "We have a new campaign that just launched this week. We're trying to restore a network of ravine wetlands throughout the city that are on a migratory path for native songbirds."

"So the little birdies have a home?"

She pursed her lips. It was hard not to stare at her mouth while she talked. It really was an unnatural shade of pink. "That is correct, though the ravines are home to lots of other wildlife, too. We're in need of a lead donation to really kick off the project with a splash."

"Are you extorting me?"

She raised her eyebrows, as if to challenge him. "You

started it. You know, what with the *blackmail*."

Damn, this woman had chutzpah. People didn't usually talk to him like this. Actually, people *never* talked to him like this. He had a feeling Rose was what they called irrepressible. That wasn't a quality the women in his social circle had in abundance. Which meant his father was going to go apeshit when he met her. "You tell me where to pick you up Saturday, and I'll bring my checkbook." This was going to be worth every penny.

She narrowed her eyes then, suspicious, as if he'd pulled one over on her even though he'd just agreed to her terms. "Does this suddenly seem a little, I don't know, unsavory?"

"You mean like prostitution?"

"God! No! Well…yes."

"Think of the birdies." He handed her his phone. "Enter your contact info."

"Oh, no!" she exclaimed, looking at the display on his phone. "Is that the time?"

"You have somewhere to be?" he asked as she entered her info, tossed him the phone, and began shutting down her computer.

"Yes! A date. In five minutes. Damn! I hate being late."

That would explain the bright lips and heavy eye makeup. He let his eyes slide down her body. And the aqua sequined top, tight jeans that hugged her curves, and lime green heels. All the bright colors stood in dramatic contrast to the curtain of straight, black hair that hung to the middle of her back and, in the front, Bettie-Page-style curled bangs. "Somehow, I think your boyfriend will be inclined to forgive."

"Oh, TallDoctor83 isn't my boyfriend. Yet."

"Right." He let his gaze flicker down to the letter, which

was still lying on the desk. "TallDoctor83 is tonight's Mr. Thursday Night. Here's hoping you don't incite your date to vomit this time. Do you go out every Thursday night?"

"Yes, I do." She snatched the letter and shoved it in her purse. "Internet dating is, alas, the way of the modern world."

"Well, there *is* always blackmail." He'd been going for a hint of levity, thinking maybe it was time to stop being so overtly rude now that he'd gotten what he wanted, but she just glared, shooed him out of her office, and locked the door. "I have a car," he said. "Let me drop you off."

She shot him a skeptical look. "That would be great, actually. Cabs are impossible this time of day, and I *really* hate being late."

They descended the stairs silently, and when his car pulled up to the curb, she planted a hand on her hip. "You have a driver." When he didn't answer, she rolled her eyes and added, "Of course you do."

He held the door open for her and slid into the backseat next to her. "Nate, we're taking this lovely lady to…"

"The Thompson Hotel," she said.

"Nice. So, let me take a wild guess. Your date is a doctor. A tall one."

She didn't answer, just looked at Nate and inclined her head a little. He forgot sometimes that the trappings of his lifestyle weren't normal for everyone. "Oh, he's sworn to secrecy, aren't you, Nate?"

"Yes indeed," his longtime driver replied.

"Still," he said, reaching for the button that raised a tinted glass partition between the front and back seats. "If you want privacy, we can do this."

"Sorry, Nate!" she called. Then she whirled on him and

said, "A chauffeur? *Really*? You're, like, the one percent, aren't you?"

He shrugged. To him, it was a simple cost-benefit analysis. He had clients all over the region, and he spent a lot of time in the car. Given what he billed hourly, if he could use that time to work, Nate's salary more than paid for itself. Plus, it was good for impressing women.

Usually.

The one next to him just snorted in what appeared to be disdain. Damn, Rose Verma just said whatever she wanted, reacted however she wanted, context be damned, didn't she? He had chosen well.

"So, TallDoctor83," he said. "If 1983 is his birth year, that makes him, what? A little older than you?"

"I'm ByAnyOtherName86, if you're fishing for my age."

A rose by any other name would smell as sweet. "Clever," he said.

"Though no one ever gets the reference. I've gone out every Thursday night for the past year, and it's only been commented on twice. And both times the guys thought *Romeo and Juliet* was romantic. I was like, dudes, they were *teenagers*, and they *died*."

He leaned in while she was babbling and sniffed the air near her neck—which caused the fuchsia mouth to clamp shut. "You *do* smell good." It was true. He couldn't place the scent, but he liked it. It was bold, almost herbal. A refreshing change from the heavy floral scents the women in his family's social circle favored.

She burst out laughing at that, which discombobulated him momentarily, as it was not the reaction he expected. "Perhaps your date will be literate as well as tall," he said.

"I don't have high hopes, to be honest." She sighed and fell back theatrically against the back of the seat. "Well, that's not true. I *always* have high hopes. It's just that they're usually dashed. I can count on one hand the number of second dates I've gone on over the past year. I had one guy that lasted three weeks, which is a record."

Rose Verma definitely came from the other side of the tracks. In addition to smelling different than the women in his social circle, she also possessed a kind of chatty forthrightness that the careful, sophisticated women he knew wouldn't be caught dead displaying. "What happened to him?" he couldn't resist asking, though small talk wasn't really his thing.

"Oh, what happened to him is that his *wife* found out about us, and I believe she cut off his balls."

He whistled.

"Yeah. I'd thought of every possible question you might want to ask a person you met on a dating site, but somehow 'Are you married?' slipped my mind."

"Why do you keep at it?" Internet dating seemed so undignified. "Why not just meet someone in the actual world?" He wasn't the relationship type, but all the women he casually dated, he met through friends or at parties.

When she didn't speak right away, he thought maybe she wasn't going to answer. But then she sighed and said, "I have no idea why I'm telling you this, but years ago, I told my mother that when I turned thirty, if I was still single, I'd let her fix me up. My birthday is in a couple months, and that is *not* a road I want to go down. So my clock is ticking. Some people have a biological clock. I have a boyfriend clock."

He almost laughed. Her mother sounded not unlike his

father. Of course, Rose's mother probably wasn't a sociopath. "So hope springs eternal."

She squared her shoulders and smiled. "It does. God knows why, but it does."

They'd pulled up in front of the hotel. "Do you have a dress? For Saturday, I mean? It's black tie."

"Yes, I have a dress," she shot back. "We can't all be the one percent, but I'm not a *total* peasant."

He held his hands up in a gesture of surrender. She was prickly, this one. All the better to stick it to dear old Dad. "All right, I'll pick you up at six."

"Don't you mean Nate will pick me up at six?" When he didn't answer, she just shook her head. "Thanks for the ride. This has been…really, really weird."

Chapter Two

It was nearly eleven by the time Rosie got home. She wanted more than anything to text Jo, to order up some sympathetic righteous indignation, but she was sensitive about the new mom's exhaustion. Her friend had been going to bed with the baby these days, and even with the Toronto-Vancouver time difference, Rosie feared waking them.

There was also the part where she sounded like a broken record every Thursday night.

Her phone buzzed as she unlocked the door. Oh! Sometimes when baby Toby woke Jo, Jo texted to see how Rosie was doing. But no—she didn't recognize the number as she fumbled her phone out of her bag.

How's it going with TallDoc?

Huh? It wasn't Jo or Hailey, the only people who knew the specifics of tonight's date.

Sorry to interrupt, but you forgot to give me your address. I only have this number, and I'm not letting you off the hook that easily.

Holy crap. She *had* forgotten to put her address in Marcus Rosemann's phone. Usually when exchanging info with a guy, it was just email and phone numbers. She pecked out her address as she stood in her entryway, fingers suddenly clumsy. Then she added:

As for TallDoc, he didn't BLACKMAIL me, but that's about all I can say for him.

Crap. That had been too bold, hadn't it? Too cheeky. This was EcoHabitat Angel Donor Rebecca Rosemann's son, after all. And he was a major EcoHabitat donor in his own right, something Rosie had managed to forget as she'd babbled at him earlier in his car. Was she *trying* to get herself fired?

Well, we all have our own signature moves. Not everybody is as accomplished at blackmail as I am.

She laughed out loud at that. A self-deprecating joke? It seemed so at odds with the taciturn man she'd met earlier. Should she reply? Well, why not? Via text, he seemed less threatening than in person, and he *had* texted her first. Sometimes a girl had to seize a venting opportunity when it presented itself.

He was actually kind of a racist misogynist masquerading as a normal human being. So he made blackmail look pretty good.

The phone rang.

Holy crap! What was he doing? "Hello?"

"Did you get home all right?" His voice was like his salt-and-pepper five o'clock shadow—rough and smooth at the same time, simultaneously dark and light.

"Yeah. I'm just getting in." She kicked off her heels, unbuttoned the top of her jeans—hello, dignity!—and flopped onto the couch.

"What happened?"

She sighed. "Well, first of all, he was not tall. I'm tall."

"I know."

"What is that supposed to mean?"

"It doesn't mean anything. It means I noticed the physiological fact that you are taller than the average woman."

Oh. She might have overreacted there. She was sensitive about her height, but that was no reason to bite his head off. "I'm five foot ten, and I was eye-to-eye with this guy. Now, I would not say that a man who's five-ten is short, per se."

"But for an attribute to make it into a screen name, it should be an obvious attribute."

"Exactly!" She plumped up the pillows behind her.

"So the guy was exaggerating—he was probably insecure. Let's get to the bigot part."

"Okay, so, we order drinks, and right away he starts negging me."

"Negging? Help me out here."

"It's when a guy hits on you by insulting you," she explained. "He might say something like, 'You'd look really pretty if you didn't have those bangs.' It's a play on the word negativity, I suppose."

"Does that work?"

"Not on me! It's supposed to, like, break down your self-esteem and make you more vulnerable to his advances because you want to win his approval. It's part of this whole Pick-Up Artist system. There are books about it. Seminars."

"Wow, that makes me feel old."

She was curious. "So, you're, what, OnePercent80?" She was underestimating, but when fishing for someone's age, underestimation seemed prudent.

"Let's just say I'm old enough to know how to be polite to my dates."

Nice dodge. Clearly, she wasn't going to find out how old he was unless she outright asked, which, even though she was being uncharacteristically forthright with him, she wasn't quite prepared to do. So she went back to her story. "Wait, it gets better. And by better I mean *worse*. He starts talking about how I'm not what he pictured from our emails. Of course, I rise to the bait and ask him what he means. He says he pictured me showing up wearing a little black dress. You know, something timeless, he said. Something *classy*."

"No."

Rosie grinned. It was like she was talking to a different man than the one who'd appeared in her office earlier. This easy, open conversation was almost as good as texting with Jo. Apparently, all she needed after one of these horrific dates was a sympathetic ear. Maybe she should get a shrink. "Yeah. And as I was sitting there kind of stunned, trying to think what to say, he told me that he would have thought, *given my heritage*, that I would shy away from such stereo-typically bright colors. I continued to look at him blankly, and he went on with this long-winded explanation about how I was wearing so many different bright colors, and they reminded him of Bollywood and saris, and he wouldn't have thought I'd want to play into that ethnic stereotype. He thought of the Thompson as a more upscale place. You know, more subdued. And then, the cherry on top was when he added that *given my size*, he would have thought I'd stick with neutral colors and classic silhouettes."

"What a fucking idiot." The disdain in his voice electrified her. She felt it like pinpricks at the surface of her skin. "So then what did you do?"

Then I started to cry. No, she couldn't tell him that. That was the difference between Marcus Rosemann and Jo. She could tell her best friend the truth, but she didn't want this slick stranger, even though at the moment he seemed sympathetic, to think she was the kind of woman who let raving assholes like TallDoctor wound her so deeply. "I, ah, went to the bathroom." That much was true. Crap, maybe she *should* get a shrink because it was probably worth noting that she had also cried in the bathroom at least once a week in seventh and eighth grade. After Jo left town, things had been pretty tough for a while there. She cleared her throat. "I needed a moment. I should have just left at that point, but I guess..."

"What?" His voice was low, extra raspy.

"I guess the negging sort of worked for a minute." She didn't want his pity, so she kept talking, lest he feel she was setting him up to have to object. "But then I got control of myself. I went back to the table, and he had ordered me another drink. At that point, I could have used it, but, even though I was probably being overly paranoid, I wasn't going to drink anything that had been out of my sight."

"I hope you poured it over his head."

She wished she had, too. The truth was, she hadn't been

brave enough. "I just turned around and walked out. Of course, he called all sorts of lovely things after me, mostly to do with the temperature of my lady parts."

"Sonofabitch."

"Yeah. Suddenly, the barfer from last week doesn't seem so bad. At least he *liked* me. He even told me I was pretty before that fateful last drink."

"You *are* pretty."

The words summoned the electricity again, except this time, instead of pinpricks, it was a lightning bolt down her spine. *You're pretty, too.* She bit her tongue. What she really wanted to do was ask him why he had called. But that seemed rude. "So this thing Saturday."

"The Fall Ball."

"Yeah, which, no offense to your mother, is kind of a dumb name."

"The name actually began as a joke. She and my aunts started it twenty-plus years ago because they wanted to raise money for a hospital that had taken good care of their mother in her final months."

Rosie refrained from saying that when normal people wanted to raise money for a cause, they got their friends to give them twenty bucks and ran a 5K race dressed in a pink tutu.

"They decided on a ball in October. While they were trying to think of a catchy name, they called it the Fall Ball. It was meant to be a placeholder, a joke, but it stuck. Its straightforwardness appealed to my mother, I think. She was a practical woman who didn't pull punches."

Rosie heard something in his voice. Not quite wistfulness—she was pretty sure Marcus Rosemann didn't do wistful—but a slight softening of his tone. "This would be the first ball since she died, right?" she asked.

He cleared his throat. "Yeah. I'm expected to bring a date, and I…"

"Decided to bribe a random stranger? I understand."

He laughed, and she felt absurdly proud to have been the cause. "I don't do relationships," he said, "so bribing random strangers suits me just fine."

Rich people were so strange. "What do you mean you don't do relationships? Like, as a matter of principle?"

He was silent for a moment, and she wondered if she'd overstepped, mistaken the odd openness of their conversation for real intimacy. It was hard to know where the boundaries were with a guy who'd blackmailed you to get you to go out with him, inspiring you to extort him in return, but then called to make sure you got home okay after a date with someone else.

"It's just not the way I'm wired," he said. "I date, sometimes, though. I'm not a monk. I just keep it casual. I'm like you—lots of first dates."

"Except I'm actually trying to find someone who sticks," said Rose. Maybe it was naive, but she still believed in happily ever after. She had worked hard to get over her childhood bullying, had created a pretty excellent life for herself, and now she wanted to share it with someone.

"Anyway," he said, interrupting her self-analysis, "after hearing about TallDoctor, I'm starting to think I overstepped this afternoon."

"Nah. Your brand of elitist, entitled arrogance was different." She was teasing, of course, but it was true. Hard to say why, though. Marcus Rosemann was clearly a man who took what he wanted and assumed the world would bend to his will. Maybe the difference was that the world *did* bend to his will. She was going with him to the damned Fall Ball, wasn't she? She was even kind of…well, *excited* was too strong a word, but it certainly would make the weekend more eventful than usual. "So," she said, when the silence on the line started to get a little uncomfortable. "Text me your email address, and I'll send you some info on the ravine project."

"The ravine project?"

"The birdies, remember? I'm extorting you?"

He barked a laugh, another genuine-sounding one that warmed her insides. "Right. You got it, Rose Verma."

After they hung up, she felt lighter than she had ten minutes ago. TallDoctor had receded into the background. By tomorrow, he'd be forgotten completely. With a sigh, she hoisted herself off the sofa to get ready for bed. That whole conversation had been so…weird.

Why did she leave every encounter with Marcus Rose-mann searching for adjectives and settling on *weird*?

"That same old shit is not going to fly here."

The room went silent. Marcus rubbed his tem-ples. He looked around the war room. His best people—sup-posedly—were congregated to work on the pitch for Mag-nifique Cosmetics. If they could snag the Canadian account of the multinational cosmetics giant, it would put the agency on the path to the global big leagues. But with the ideas he was being shown, the Rosemann Agency was destined to be forever mired in the Canadian medium leagues, toiling away on fast food, batteries, and banks.

"I think what Marcus is trying to say," said Lauren, his executive creative director, "is that lipstick is different from burgers."

What he *wanted* to say was that when he was starting the company from nothing, against his family's wishes, toiling away with Lauren in a tiny rented office they couldn't afford, he had treated every pitch like it was the only thing standing between him and destitution—because it had been, unless he'd wanted to go crawling back to his father. Now, he had luxurious office space in the Lakefront Centre to house an army of staff, and this was the crap they were giving him? Everyone had gone soft.

He let his hand fall to the table, and it thudded harder than he'd expected. Several among the group jumped in their seats. Were they so tender that they couldn't take a little show of annoyance? He let the other hand fall. One of the copywriters sitting next to him rolled her chair away a few inches.

"Guys, can you give us the room for a moment?" Lauren said.

The assembled staff, apparently all too happy to comply, hurried out.

"I should have put you on this," Marcus said. Lauren was working all out on a Mercedes campaign they'd recently snagged as part of their attempt to diversify the firm's client base, so they'd had one of the art directors who worked under her get started on the Magnifique project. But obviously that had been a tactical error, and either he or Lauren should have been babysitting the project from the start.

"Okay, first off, calm down."

"I am calm."

"You are not calm. Take a breath."

He glared at her. She was always telling him to breathe.

"We agreed that since I know shit-all about makeup, Jody would oversee this stage. I don't know bronzer from BB cream. I'm purely a moisturize, mascara, and go kind of person."

He scowled. "I don't wear makeup at all," he said, "but I don't need to to know that close-ups of lips are not going to cut it, no matter who their celebrity spokespeople are." Jody was a relatively new employee who worked on Lauren's team. What had he been thinking leaving something so important with someone so untested? He flipped through an issue of *Cosmopolitan* lying on the table. "The crap they're proposing looks like every single ad in here."

"Right. But your Angry Boss act isn't helping."

"I'm not acting." They were going to get the Magnifique account if he had to personally bullwhip each and every one of his employees daily until the bid, which was just over three weeks away.

"I actually have an idea. Wanna hear it?"

He sighed. "All right. Can't be any worse than that stuff."

Lauren had a way of defusing tense situations. The smartest thing he'd ever done with the company was to bring her on board. After the first year of going it alone, once he'd managed to land a couple long-term clients, he'd reached out to his old university pal. She had been a radical art major and he a straight-laced economics major. After he'd tried to pick her up in a bar, she'd given him a sound dressing down, informing him that even if she hadn't been a lesbian, he was the last person in the world she would date. From there, an unlikely but fast friendship blossomed, and together they'd built the Rosemann Agency into a lucrative, successful business.

Even if it was built on cheeseburgers and chicken nuggets.

"Give me five minutes to get my head together," she said.

Marcus spent those five minutes making a donation to Rose's save the birds thing. Since EcoHabitat had been one of his mother's favorite charities, he didn't lowball it. Besides, he could just imagine Rose's face when she found out. Maybe for one second, it would wipe that smart-alecky expression off her face. Make that pink-lipped jaw drop.

"Okay, take two," Lauren said, leading everyone back into the conference room. Marcus looked at Jody, who was looking at the floor. Good. She was going to have to pull her socks up if she wanted to last here. "As we all know," Lauren started, "Magnifique is looking to update its image."

It was true. The brief the company had shared with Marcus and the competing agencies had stated a desire to reach urban women in their twenties and early thirties. The company's core customer was currently in her late thirties or early forties.

"With that in mind," said Lauren, "how about a series of ads for Magnifique's long-wearing lipstick? We show models doing things that are a bit edgy—for example, making out with a guy in a semi-public location. On an inset, we show two close-ups of the guy's collar. One has the telltale lipstick smudge on it, and the other does not. Of course, the model wearing Magnifique is the one whose lipstick hasn't transferred. Another ad does the same thing with a burger. One burger has a bite out of it with a big lipstick print on the bun, whereas there's no evidence on the Magnifique one. We shoot everything very cinema-verite, American Apparel-esque, like these models are actually being caught doing something transgressive."

He smiled. The irony was not lost on him. The idea of using the dreaded fast-food burger in this coveted high-end campaign, should they be awarded the job, tickled his funny bone. He tapped his fingers on the table, enjoying that subtle buzzing sensation that always overtook him when a concept was good. "Get a group together and run with this. I need to see something in twenty-four hours." He glanced at his watch as the room began to hum with conversation. He'd be on the way to the Fall Ball in twenty-four hours. "Nope, sooner. Courier mock-ups to my house by three o'clock tomorrow."

Maybe he'd even see what Rose Verma, fuchsia-lipped single urban girl, thought about the concept.

"What the *heck*?" Rosie reared back from her phone as she sat at a conference table at work, waiting for a meeting to start, drawing Hailey's attention from where she was setting up the projector for Rosie's presentation. "Look at this donation we just got for the wetlands project!"

"Holy shit! Fifty grand? Who is it from?"

"I'm looking," she said, scrolling through the email from their very excited donations processor, but she already knew. When she'd sent Marcus the link—well, when she'd *extorted* him—she'd thought he might pony up a grand or two. But this. This was beyond her imaginings.

Mr. Carroll strolled into the room eating a sandwich. In addition to being incompetent, their boss was so…gross. Rosie was convinced that he was one of those people who were so bad at their jobs that they actually ended up rewarded for it—one organization turfed him, and he went on to a bigger job at another. He'd cut a swath through the Toronto nonprofit sector, and now EcoHabitat was stuck with him. In the meantime, she was trying to minimize the damage, because unlike him, she actually cared about what they were trying to do.

He sighed and lowered himself into a chair as if the effort was too much. The fifty-something executive director seemed a decade older than his years—hence everyone's habit of addressing him formally as Mr. "Are we ready, then?" he asked through a mouthful of pastrami.

"We are." Rosie smiled at him and the handful of others who had joined them at the table. She was making a case that EcoHabitat needed a new website. "Let's get started."

"I just don't see what the problem with the current site is," Mr. Carroll said after having chomped his way through her thoughtfully prepared and meticulously argued presentation.

Had he even heard a word she said? "Well, as I demonstrated in the presentation," she said with a forced smile, "the navigation isn't always clear, and a person has to click through a lot of levels to get information about any of our projects—or, perhaps more critically, to make a donation."

"Some of the photography is looking a little dated, too," said Jill, their scientific advisor, aka, the Person Who Actually Knew Stuff. She had a PhD in evolutionary biology and was smarter than the rest of them put together.

Thank you, Dr. Jill! "I agree. We clearly have both architectural and artistic challenges to overcome." Rosie wished she had the skills to just redo the site herself in a kind of guerilla redesign. "Perhaps I could take the next step of putting together a project brief and soliciting quotes from some design firms."

Hailey, who had been taking notes in the corner, glared at Rosie. She was forever pointing out when Rosie took on tasks that weren't part of her job description. But if Rosie limited herself to what was in her job description, a) nothing would ever get done at the charity, and b) she'd be stuck in her office writing thank-you letters to rich people all day.

Or writing letters to her best friend and mistakenly sending them to rich people. Whatever.

Thinking about rich people made her think about Marcus. After they'd gotten off the phone last night, she'd tried on every dress in her closet. When he had first invited her to the ball, she'd actually thought she would wear a swishy, classic black number, but since TallDoctor had made that little black dress remark, she felt as if to do so would be giving in somehow. She didn't want Marcus to think she was taking TallDoctor's criticism to heart. Which was stupid because it wasn't like she and Marcus were ever going to see each other again after the ball, so who cared what he thought? He'd asked her on some kind of strange power-tripping whim, and they didn't exactly run in the same circles.

Still. She couldn't get his voice out of her head, all low and raspy as she was curled up in the dark last night. *You are pretty.*

Time to go shopping.

Chapter Three

"I'll be right down," Rose called through the intercom in the foyer of her building.

Marcus shifted the flowers he was carrying so he could press the talk button. She probably didn't want a virtual stranger knowing exactly where she lived, but he didn't care. "Nope, I'm coming up. I have something for you. What number?"

There was a pause, but then she said, "Twelfth floor. 1206."

His knock set off a flurry of barking. He hadn't quite figured her for a dog person. Having spent the afternoon looking at the new Magnifique mock-ups— which, to his great relief, were showing a lot of promise—he'd been thinking about the hypothetical younger Magnifique customer they were trying to reach. Which really meant he'd been thinking about Rose. She seemed like the type—young, single downtowner with a distinct sense of style. He just hadn't pictured a dog.

"Fifi! Shhh!" She swung open the door with one hand while holding the dog by the collar with the other.

He *certainly* hadn't pictured an overweight beagle named Fifi. He would have laughed at the incongruous name, but the impulse died in his throat when he caught a glimpse of Rose. TallDoctor hadn't been wrong when he'd told her she dressed like someone out of a Bollywood film. Not because she was Indian, but because she *was* into color. She was wearing a teal and silver striped mini dress made out of some kind of shiny fabric. Its fitted, V-neck bodice hugged her breasts, and the skirt stopped just above her knees. Her ruby-red patent leather high heels were like a pair of exclamation points.

"You clean up pretty well, Rose Verma," he said, understating the matter entirely. If he was also pleased that her dress would raise a few eyebrows at the staid ball, he didn't let on.

She grinned. "Thanks." Her smile withered though, as Fifi let loose a mournful houndish howl.

"So, this is…Fifi?" he asked, staring down the beast, who eyed him warily.

"Yes. I'm fostering her—she just arrived today. I do that sometimes—keep animals temporarily when there aren't any shelter spaces free in the city."

"That's…nice." What could he say? He wasn't an animal person.

"It started a few years ago when someone dumped a cat in a crate on the front steps of EcoHabitat. I guess they knew that wildlife conservation was part of our mission."

"The common housecat being an excellent example of

the sort of wildlife you're intent on saving."

"Yeah, well, I tried to take it to the Humane Society, but they were full. I finally found a shelter that said they might have a spot in a week's time, so I kept the cat until then. Then they—the people at this shelter—sort of got me on their radar. Fifi, sit!"

"You're a sucker, is what you're saying." He'd meant it as a factual observation, but to his surprise, it came out like he was trying to tease her.

"That's exactly what I'm saying." She grinned sheepishly. "But it works out. I love animals. Realistically, I can't have a dog in a high-rise like this. It wouldn't be fair to the dog. But it's obviously better for them to spend a few weeks here in less-than-ideal circumstances than to be put down. The best part is that I get to name them, and—oh!" She'd been so consumed with wrangling Fifi that she hadn't really looked at him. Her lips, which were painted scarlet today—to match her shoes, perhaps—rounded into an *O* of surprise. "Are those for me?"

He handed over the bouquet.

"Thank you—they're beautiful. Peonies are my favorite."

He felt a ping of satisfaction that his instructions to Carla to produce something pink and over-the-top—but not roses—had hit the mark. "I figured that when you're named Rose, probably everyone brings you roses."

"I don't think bringing flowers to a date is really a thing anymore." She paused, then added, "Not that this is a date."

"Right," he agreed, checking out her apartment while she was in the kitchen. "This is blackmail." As she laughed—and Fifi eyed him—he took in the space that was as colorful as her clothing. From where he stood in the entryway, he could see through to a dining-living room combination. A small glass café table was flanked by two teal upholstered chairs, and beyond that, the living room featured a bright white sofa covered with dozens of throw pillows in vibrant, contrasting colors and patterns. Rose, she was Too Much. In other words: ideal.

"Ready?" She appeared at his side.

Damn. Now that she wasn't struggling with Fifi, he could get a proper look at her and not just her clothing. Her hair had been shaped into waves that fell around her shoulders, and her soulful, amber-flecked brown eyes were fringed by what might be the world's prettiest eyelashes. His conclusion: In addition to being rude and boorish, TallDoctor was a simpleton. Because Rose was stunning. If you went for that kind of thing. "Do you use long-wearing lipstick?" he asked.

"Huh?" A hand flew to her dark red mouth. "Dude, are you going to start negging me, too?"

"No. My agency is pitching to a cosmetics company. We're presenting concepts for a campaign for their long-wearing lipstick. So I have a newfound interest in what people wear on their lips. Especially stylish young urbanites such as yourself. You're exactly the sort of customer they're trying to reach."

"Ah!" She ushered him out the door and locked it. "Nope, this is just several layers of regular lipstick. I generally find the long-wearing stuff too drying."

"If you don't mind, I'll show you some concepts in the car, see what you think."

She clapped her hands as they stepped into the elevator. "Fun!" Then, a few minutes later, she stepped into the car, calling "Hi, Nate!" over the half-lowered partition, causing the usually taciturn chauffeur to smile at her in the rearview mirror. Nobody who rode in his car ever spoke to Nate. In his world, people were polite but distant with employees.

Marcus slid in next to Rose, unzipped the leather portfolio containing the mock-ups, and slid the first one over.

"Oh, funny!" Her face lit up as she took in the two cheeseburgers—one lipstick stained, the other not. Then, in a flash, delight was replaced by dismay as she wrinkled her nose and furrowed her brow. "Oh, no." She made a theatrical choking sound. "Magnifique tests on animals." She let the paper fall to her lap, as if touching it would somehow contaminate her. "Don't roll your eyes at me."

He hadn't even realized he'd done it, but being scolded for it made him do it again.

"They're one of the worst offenders on that front, actually."

His eyes had barely flickered down to her red shoes before she said, "And don't make a crack about my shoes. Leather is different." He just raised his eyebrows. "It *is*. I've had these shoes for *years*."

"But you liked the ad, didn't you?"

"It doesn't matter how good the ad is. I would never buy anything from Magnifique."

Alrighty then. He slid the offending mock-up into the portfolio and sat back to marinate in the uncomfortable silence that had overtaken them. He'd been planning to fill her in about his family before they got to the ball. Not about how his tyrant of a father would be irritated as hell by her presence—not about how he'd invited her for that very reason—but enough that she wouldn't be blindsided.

But screw it. They would just wing it.

The ballroom at the Four Seasons was spectacular. Of course it was. But it was an understated sort of spectacular, with its wraparound windows and white, satin-dressed tables. In fact, it made Rosie wonder if TallDoctor's advice to dress more sedately hadn't been so far off—maybe a safe little black dress would have been the better choice in this refined setting. As it was, even though the ball had not officially started, she was already feeling like The Girl Who Didn't Get the Memo. The handful of women here this early all wore floor-length gowns in black, gray, or the odd jewel tone.

She didn't have enough time to really fret about it, though, because they hadn't been in the room ten seconds before a pair of older women descended upon them. For a moment, she had a flashback of being in the hallway in seventh grade at Aurora Heights Public School, Tiffany and Ashley and their henchwomen approaching. It had only been two years—once Rosie hit high school, she'd found a couple like-minded artsy kids and hit her stride. But those two years after Jo left had marked her. Apparently more than she'd even realized, given how quickly her mind went back there at moments of vulnerability.

"Marcus, you did bring someone!" said one of the women, doing a quick scan of Rosie. She and her companion, who could have been twins, were striking, slender, and silver-haired. Was it her imagination, or did the two women share a knowing glance, something that conveyed just the slightest hint of disapproval? Rosie ran her hands up and down her dress. She definitely should have gone with black.

"Well, if it isn't the black sheep of the family." A man joined their circle and clasped Marcus on the shoulder, his warm, friendly grin signaling that he was teasing. He looked a lot like Marcus—he had those killer blue-gray eyes—but younger. It was hard to pinpoint why, but when he turned his attention to Rosie and raised his eyebrows, his scrutiny was entirely different from that of the women. He seemed amused, but not at Rosie's expense. "And who is *this*?"

Marcus turned to her. "Rose, these are my aunts, Ruth and Rachel, and my cousin, Cary. Everyone, this is Rose Verma."

Rosie shook all the hands offered to her, stifling an absurd impulse to curtsy. The women all seemed so poised and polished, like Tiffany and Ashley fast forwarded forty or fifty years.

"My aunts founded this ball along with my mother," Marcus said.

"It won't be the same without Rebecca," said Ruth, folding Marcus into a hug. Rosie watched him resist for a long moment, then soften and permit the embrace.

"Everything is beautiful," said Rosie.

Rachel—the aunt who wasn't hugging Marcus—peered at Rosie over a pair of gold spectacles. "And where did you meet Marcus?"

Marcus stepped back from the circle and took Rosie's arm. "Rose works at EcoHabitat," he said, as if this explained anything.

But it did seem to have a mollifying effect because both aunts smiled. "Such a good cause and so close to Rebecca's heart," Ruth said.

"We appreciated her leadership so much," Rosie said, sneaking a glance at the cousin, Cary, who had been eyeing her openly this whole time.

"Have you and Marcus been dating long?" Cary asked. There was nothing overtly suspicious about his tone, but Rosie felt like the question was loaded somehow.

"Not too long," said Marcus, preempting any answer she might have made and pulling her tighter to his side. "But sometimes, you just know."

Whaaaat?

Cary narrowed his eyes. "Rose, has Marcus told you about his father?"

She turned to Marcus. "I'm not sure. I—"

"*Marcus*," Cary said, his open, friendly countenance transforming instantly into something much less benign.

"Let's hit the bar," Marcus said, tugging Rosie's arm.

All three of his relatives shared another one of those cryptic looks but let the matter drop.

Rosie, however, was not planning to. "What about your father?" she asked as they departed.

"It's nothing, really. We just don't have the best relationship."

She dug in her heels, halting their progress. "You tell me what the hell is going on, or I'm leaving."

Silent, he met her eyes for a long time.

"I'm not kidding," she said. She wasn't planning on spending the evening with the terse, borderline-rude version of Marcus she'd met in her office. She'd had a hint on the phone last night of a warmer, almost sensitive man beneath the brusque exterior, and she'd rather do her time with *that* Marcus.

He sighed. "All right. Here's the short version: My father is a tyrant who rules this family with an iron fist. I am a perpetual disappointment to him for many reasons, chief among them that I won't come back to the family firm and that I won't settle down and marry a nice Jewish girl."

She almost laughed because, oh, could she ever relate to that. She sometimes feared that her mother's threats to "fix her up" if she was still single at thirty would snowball into an arranged marriage. The prospect of her mother finding her a boyfriend was worse than when they'd first moved to Canada and her well-meaning first grade teacher had "assigned" a few girls to be her friends—before she and Jo had become best friends at first sight. "So if your father's goal in life is for you to marry a nice Jewish girl, then why am I here?"

"*My* goal in life is to annoy the shit out of my father."

Everything suddenly made a sickening sort of sense. Marcus's appearance in her office. His strange insistence that she accompany him to the ball. He'd brought her here *because* she didn't know what kind of dress to wear. The sheer offensiveness of it almost took her breath away. "So you're using me," she said, hating the way her voice came out a little shaky.

"Of course I'm using you," he said evenly, as if he were commenting on the weather. "Are you forgetting the part where your presence here is the result of blackmail?"

Right. What had she thought? That someone like Marcus Rosemann would meet someone like her and be inspired to impulsively ask her out just because? She lifted her chin, just as her mom had taught her to do back in the day. "In addition to being astonishingly rude, this scheme is awfully immature. You're a grown-up. A very successful one. Why let your father get to you?"

He looked away, and she could sense that he was about to clam up again.

What a complete bastard. "All right, that's it. I'm out."

Just as she was turning to leave, he answered, voice clipped. "*He* doesn't think I'm successful. He never forgave me for starting the ad agency—cut me off, in fact, just after university." He stopped, but she sensed there was more there, and her silence was rewarded: "I was supposed to succeed him at the family investment counsel. But instead he's stuck with Cary—though I shouldn't say stuck. He's a financial genius. Much better at it than I ever would have been. But my father still thinks I'm going to come to my senses, see the agency was just a little rebellion, and—"

"Join the investment firm and marry a nice Jewish girl."

His jaw flexed. "Something like that."

"And you're gleefully disappointing him every step of the way. Thumbing your nose at him with the girl from the other side of the tracks who's wearing the crazy minidress. You brought me here because I'm totally inappropriate."

"Inappropriate is in the eye of the beholder. I think you're very appropriate." He eyed her with undisguised appreciation, and her cheeks began to heat. She was at war with herself. On the one hand, she should be wildly offended. She *had* been wildly offended. But although this whole scheme of Marcus's was totally screwed up, it also didn't seem like he meant her any harm. He was a player, for sure, but he wasn't playing *her*. He'd actually been nothing but honest with her about who he was. Pressing his hand to the small of her back, he started them moving again. He bent over to whisper in her ear, "Come have a drink with me, and then you can go."

She nodded, feeling distinctly like the proverbial deer caught in headlights as she let him guide her through the thickening crowd. He smiled at people as they passed. Many of them looked like they wanted to stop and talk, but Marcus had a way of commanding a room, and its inhabitants, so that he could move through it at will, nothing sticking to him. It was very…impressive.

"In fact, you make everyone here look like they're still back in Kansas while you're in Technicolor Oz," he said, still whispering as they walked. "I wouldn't call that inappropriate."

She searched for a casual response, one that wouldn't give away the fact that his proximity, the authority he projected, made her heart race. "Oddly, I think that might be a nice version of what TallDoctor said to me on Thursday."

"My comment had nothing to do with your *heritage*, to use that asshole's term. Not that I presume to know what your heritage is." They'd reached a small bar tucked into a far corner of the grand ballroom. "What do you want?"

"I'll have champagne." She'd seen a couple other guests with flutes, and hey, if she was going to have a drink before she left, she was going to enjoy all the trappings for her short sojourn in this high-society fairy tale. "And," she said, addressing his previous comment, "I *am* Indian. We immigrated when I was six. My little brother was born here, so he's the first generation Canadian in our family—though we're all citizens now. My dad became a citizen a month before he died—he was so proud." She watched the bartender uncork a new bottle of Veuve Cliquot and wondered what a ticket to the ball cost if your means of entry wasn't being the inappropriate date of the host family's black sheep.

"But being Indian isn't why you like bright colors, is it? That's like saying I'm rich because I'm Jewish."

"Exactly! So I like bright colors. What can I say?" She made a self-mocking face. "I'm very stylish."

As he tucked a fifty into the bartender's tip jar, she tried not to cough on her first sip. She never tipped at these open bar things. Which obviously meant she was a peasant, despite her protestations to the contrary the other day. She was the minidress-wearing, non-tipping inappropriate girl Marcus had brought solely to bait his father. She needed to remember that, and not let him charm her into staying. She took a big gulp of her drink.

"You *are* very stylish. The perfect Magnifique woman."

"Yeah, nice try. I'd go all no-filter, makeup-free—and that's saying *a lot* for me—before I'd wear Magnifique." She hoped he would let it drop. It wasn't like she was some PETA-obsessed fringy lunatic. She just wasn't personally into hurting animals. "So why is this account so important?" she asked, waving off a server who'd approached with a platter of chicken satay.

"I'm trying to rebrand the firm," said Marcus, helping himself to a skewer. "I started from nothing, so I took every client I could get. My first big one was Crazy Bert."

"Ha! The appliance guy? Is he still around?"

"He is. And he's not the maniacal idiot he plays on TV. It's all part of his brand—a brand I did not develop but inherited, I hasten to add. He had a fight with his previous PR firm because they were trying to class him up. He was determined to hold onto the buffoon shtick."

"I guess if it works." Another server approached. Ah!

Bruschetta! Why not eat a bit before she left? That's what the inappropriate girl would do, right? Since Marcus had declined, she took two pieces, telling him, "I'm having yours."

"It *does* work, so I left it alone and delivered what he wanted—more of the same ranting TV spots and those crazy subway ads. Then I went on to snag a bunch of fast food companies. Don't get me wrong. They pay the bills. They pay the bills very nicely."

She noticed how much easier it seemed to be for him to talk about his company than it had been to talk about his family. He was positively chatty by comparison to a minute ago. "How big is your company?" she asked, finding herself genuinely interested.

"I have about a hundred and twenty employees. So not a huge global firm, but big enough."

Rosie was impressed. After all, she was a peasant. Marcus's life was so far removed from her world that she felt like she'd tumbled down the rabbit hole. The rich-people rabbit hole. Rose shook her head at an incoming server bearing a tray of mini-sliders.

"I'm sensing a pattern here, aren't I?" said Marcus. "You're a vegetarian, aren't you?" He rolled his eyes. "Of course you are." He took two of the tiny burgers. "I'm having yours, by the way."

She sighed. "Look—"

"Do you have a tiny pot of red paint in that little handbag to dump on any fur-wearing socialites?" He spoke through a mouthful of burger.

"No!"

"Because it would be kind of hilarious if you did. That really *would* make you inappropriate."

She hated that he could fluster her so easily. "I'm not one of those preachy vegetarians. It's just that for me..." God, she sounded like such a Pollyanna. When he raised his eyebrows expectantly and stuffed the other burger into his mouth, it ignited a spark of annoyance in her chest. "I figure that I live in a prosperous, enlightened society. So as much as I can, I try to make choices that don't cause other beings to suffer." There. Who cared if she sounded like a wide-eyed hippie? Even if she didn't go around shouting them from rooftops, her convictions were nothing to be ashamed of. She remembered what it was like to suffer, and there was enough suffering in the world without her adding to it.

"But what about bacon?" he asked. "How do you live without bacon?"

"I thought you were Jewish."

"I'm not that kind of Jewish. And *I* thought we were post-ethnic stereotyping, you and me."

"Touché. Anyway, I'm not saying it's not a sacrifice. I didn't spring from the heel of Zeus loving kale." He snorted. She liked that she could make him laugh. Laughing looked so incongruous on him, contrasted so much with his buttoned-up appearance and persona. It was like naming her dogs—the unexpected was sometimes a delight. "Back to your company," she said, wanting to steer the conversation away from her vegetarianism. "So you're slumming it with fast food and discount appliance warehouses, but it's paying the bills."

"Right. But I'm trying to..."

"Class up the joint?" she supplied, remembering that she was supposed to be drinking and running. She took another gulp of the Veuve, enjoying the way it made the fist inside her unclench a bit.

"Yeah. Sounds kind of snobbish, but it's true."

"No. I get it. We do it at EcoHabitat, too. We try to get donations from certain tastemakers. Not necessarily rich people, so they're not big donations per se, but cool people, you know? Then it's like we're cool by association."

"Exactly," he said. "We snagged a Mercedes campaign recently, which was great. But Magnifique's expansion into Canada—that would be huge for us. They have three firms pitching on a five-year print and TV contract. If we win the account, it could be the start of a new era for the company."

"Marcus!"

"And speak of the devil," Marcus muttered under his breath as he turned.

Rosie followed his gaze to see a tiny, stunning woman approaching. She looked like a younger, smaller version of Annette Benning. A strawberry blonde pixie cut framed a face with cheekbones that looked like they had been sculpted out of marble. She wore a forest green sheath—one of those dresses that look like nothing on the hanger, but on certain women, were the reason the phrase *effortless chic* existed.

Rosie was not one of those women. She would have looked like the Green Giant wearing a tent if she attempted a dress like that.

"Gail," said Marcus, his tone not cold exactly, but changed enough to make Rosie take notice. "May I introduce Rose Verma? Rose, Gail Abram is a partner in HW&A, another ad agency in town."

Gail gave Rosie her hand knuckles up, limply. Was she supposed to kiss it, for heaven's sake? "It's nice to meet you," she said, but Gail wasn't looking at Rosie.

"How's the Magnifique bid coming?" Gail pulled her hand from Rosie and rested it on Marcus's forearm. A vein popped in his temple. As Rosie downed the rest of her drink, a server appeared at her elbow with another. Wow. This really was another world. She nodded her thanks and lifted her glass to the waiter in a silent toast that made him grin. Probably she shouldn't have done that. Classy women probably didn't toast the waiter at the Fall Ball. She turned her attention back to Marcus and Tinkerbell.

"The bid is fine," Marcus was saying. "And yours?"

Gail smiled as she ran a finger up Marcus's arm, over his shoulder, and then down his lapel. "We are going to utterly crush you, Marcus."

Rosie gasped. She immediately wished she hadn't because what kind of unsophisticated hick gasped at something like that? Clearly the answer was one slightly buzzed on expensive champagne. But on the other hand, *we are going to utterly crush you?* This Gail chick talked like a comic-book villain, so maybe the gasp hadn't been completely off the mark.

But it had caused Gail to swing her now-bemused attention to Rosie. "So you're one of Marcus's girls?"

Marcus put his arm around Rosie's waist. She knew it was just for show, but it felt…nice. Surprisingly solid, like it was them against Gail. Which was absurd, because everything about the evening was a facade.

"It was good to see you, Gail," Marcus said, pulling Rosie a little closer, the fine wool of his suit sliding against her bare shoulders.

Rosie couldn't stop thinking of the phrase the other

woman had used. *One of Marcus's girls.* "Nice to meet you," she managed.

Gail smirked. "Likewise."

Rosie moved to step away from Marcus as Gail retreated, but he kept hold of her.

"What?" she said, looking up at him. He had her nestled so close to him that their faces were inches away. If she just leaned up a little, their lips would be practically touching, and—

"So there's no way I can get you to stay?"

"Why would I do that?" she asked, trying to recover her composure. "Give me one good reason."

"Well, I did make that donation…" He trailed off, leaving her to fill in the blank.

The bastard. She wrenched herself out of his grasp. "Right, and you can't un-make it."

"I can do whatever I want."

He probably could. But damned if she was staying to subject herself to this outrageous charade. She might not own a pair of opera gloves, but she had as much self-respect as anyone here. "Then take your tainted money back," she whisper-yelled. "Money—even for EcoHabitat—is not going to keep me here. I am not for sale."

They stared at each other, and just like two days ago in her office, it felt like a standoff. She'd lost that one, but she wasn't giving up this time. She had barely settled in for the long haul when Marcus dropped his gaze. When he looked back up at her, his face was different—more open, somehow.

"How about staying because you would be doing me a huge favor?" He shook his head, almost as if he were disgusted with himself. "I know it's immature. You were right about that. But I just wanted to…"

She sighed. "You wanted to stick it to your father the bully." Rosie knew bullies, and she knew the feeling. *Goddammit.* She was going to cave.

Marcus looked surprised by her assessment, but before he could respond, Cary approached. "Are we ready for dinner, lovebirds?"

"I don't know," said Marcus, talking to Cary but still looking quizzically at her. "Are we?"

Rosie sighed again. "I'm going to need another glass of champagne."

The head table was full of Marcus's relatives. Rosie stood out like a sore thumb among the extended Rosemann family, with their tasteful eveningwear and hushed conversations. But hey, she thought bitterly, that was the whole point, wasn't it?

She was seated on one side of Marcus. The empty spot on his other side was meant for the notorious father, who had yet to make an appearance.

Of course, she had to be bent over trying to discreetly twist the ankle of her pantyhose so her shoe would obscure a run she'd just noticed, when the patriarch arrived.

"Marcus."

There was such coldness in his tone that Rosie froze. It was worse than Gail. Way worse than Gail. If Rosie's mother ever intoned her name with that kind of robotic disdain, she'd probably cause Rosie to burst into tears.

"Father."

Well, to be fair, Marcus's voice wasn't exactly brimming with filial love. And who actually called their father "Father?"

"This is Rose."

Oh, shit. That was her cue. And she was still bent over so the table hid her from view. She plastered a smile on her face and popped up, reeling a little from the effects of two-and-a-half glasses of champagne. Well, Marcus had wanted inappropriate.

"Rose Verma, meet my father, Bart Rosemann."

"Mr. Rosemann, it's so nice to meet you."

Marcus's father paused for a few seconds before saying, "Miss Verma."

Oh, but there were entire universes contained in that pause. It was hard to say how she could tell, but that pause signified disapproval. Disdain. Maybe even contempt. For her? Or Marcus? That, she didn't know. But either way, what a supreme jerk. He didn't even know her, and Marcus was his *child*.

Everyone at the table had grown silent. She wasn't sure if it was her presence that had caused the hush or if it was the normal effect of Marcus's father's iron fist. Either way, everyone stared at him as if he were a visiting dignitary. He played the role, too, surveying the table with a frown as if it was not quite measuring up in the personal fiefdom depart-ment. Finally, he signaled that they should begin. Rosie felt a little like she was back in seventh grade, waiting for the lunch bell to ring so she could take her food and go hide in the hallway to eat.

As everyone tucked into antipasto plates—cheese, ol-ives, and figs drizzled with honey—the tension in the air was palpable. It was funny because on the surface, nothing had happened. Marcus had introduced her to his father, and she and his father had greeted each other. But clearly everything about their relationship was below the surface. If she had been trying to explain it to someone — to Jo, for instance — it would sound daft. Because *nothing* had happened. And yet *everything* had happened.

It was also odd how she could tell that a pit of rage was boiling inside Marcus. No one else seemed to notice, but his lips were pressed more firmly together than usual, and there was that same vein popping in his temple as when they'd encountered Gail. But the father pop was *a lot* more pronounced than the Gail pop. Without thinking, she placed her hand on his forearm. Who knew what she intended? Comfort? Solidarity? He jumped a little — not enough for anyone else to notice, but enough that he followed it with a sheepish smile that made her heart twist. It was as if he was embarrassed but resigned to have been caught out being affected by his father.

"You must be very proud of Marcus," said Rosie, shifting her gaze from Marcus to his father. She couldn't resist. If she was going to play this role, why not go all out? When Mr. Rosemann turned to her, ignoring Marcus between them, and raised his eyebrows as if he were humoring a tiresome underling, she added, "Being a self-made man and all, creating such a successful company from nothing."

It wasn't that Mr. Rosemann rolled his eyes. It was nothing so obvious as that. She couldn't even put her finger on exactly what he did, but there was a subtle shift in his gaze, followed by a slight widening of his eyes. "Yes," he said, his voice still completely devoid of any inflection or emotion. It was like being lectured by a corpse. A very judgy corpse.

"Marcus is a self-made man, thanks to Burger Prince and Crazy Bert."

Rosie understood then, all of a sudden, why Marcus wanted the Magnifique account so badly. Why he was determined to refocus the firm. She wasn't sure that Marcus himself did, but it was as clear as anything to her that he was trying to show up his father. It wasn't enough that Marcus was rich and successful. The way he did it mattered.

She could also see—again, even if Marcus could not— that Mr. Rosemann was the kind of man who was never going to be impressed by anything Marcus did on his own terms.

The man was a bully, plain and simple.

And she knew bullies. The best thing to do about them was to walk away, to disengage. But she couldn't help it. She suddenly felt very much like she needed to display her loyalty to Team Marcus. Hell, she suddenly—and inexplicably, but she wasn't going to cross-examine the emotion now— felt like the *captain* of Team Marcus. So she put on her best impression of a doe-eyed, lovestruck, *inappropriate* girl and gazed at Marcus with what she hoped would be interpreted as adoration. She had a sinking feeling that what might be coming through was actually lust, though, because at that precise moment, he popped a fig into his mouth and a little dribble of honey caught in the corner of his lips. And she wanted to lick it off. She kind of understood why Marcus never had to resort to the internet for all his casual dating.

"What do you do, Miss Verma?" Mr. Rosemann asked, eyebrows raised with preemptive skepticism as if he thought she might say, "Oh, I'm a lady of the evening."

"Rose works at EcoHabitat," Marcus said before she

could answer.

"Yes," she chimed in. "We were so sorry to hear of your wife's passing. She was such a supporter of our organization."

"My wife and I were separated when she died."

Okaaay then. She hadn't known that. So the web was even more tangled than she'd realized. What a supreme jerk. The woman was dead, and he still went to pains to point out to strangers that they'd been separated?

They were saved by the arrival of an army of servers, clearing the appetizer plates and replacing them with... giant hunks of bloody steak.

Well, to be fair, they were really rather modest servings of steak, surrounded by a good-looking pile of sautéed vegetables and some roasted potatoes. This would be fine. She could scooch the steak to the side of her plate, eat the side dishes, and then drape her napkin over the uneaten meat.

Marcus's hand shot out and prevented a server from setting a plate down in front of her. "My date will need a vegetarian meal."

He spoke loudly enough that he drew the attention of everyone around them, including, of course, his father.

"It's fine," she started to protest, but Marcus cut her off.

"No, it's not fine." He swiveled to face the server. "Bring something else."

"You're a vegetarian, Miss Verma," Mr. Rosemann said. This time the not-quite-an-eye-roll was dangerously close to becoming an actual eye roll. It didn't escape her that Marcus had rolled his eyes in a dramatic fashion upon learning the same bit of news about her eating habits earlier in the evening, but somehow his father's eye roll was different. It was mean.

"Yes. Rose is a vegetarian," Marcus said, staring down his father. She knew it was all pretend, but part of her thrilled a little to be championed by a powerful man like Marcus.

Mr. Rosemann took his time sawing off a hunk of steak, popping it in his mouth, chewing, and swallowing before drawling, "Well, how chivalrous of you to champion one of your girls so vehemently."

Again with the "Marcus's girls" thing. Did the man have a *harem*?

"Rose isn't one of my girls," said Marcus.

That much was true. Wasn't and never would be.

"She's my fiancée."

Chapter Four

Rose hid her surprise well. Probably better than Marcus himself had. Because he was as dumbfounded as anyone by the astonishing sentence that had just come out of his mouth. One minute, it had been business as usual, his father aiming his signature brand of icy disdain at Marcus, Marcus trying not to blow a gasket at the Fall Ball, his mother's legacy to the world. The next, though, his father had started aiming his passive-aggressive insults at Rose, and that simply could not be allowed to stand.

Still, he wasn't quite sure why he had popped out the fiancée thing. Just that he felt, oddly, that an insult to Rose in this context was an insult to him, and it was important that his father knew it.

It's also possible that, in some part of his reptilian brain, he knew the news would be a knife to his father's heart. Because somewhere in that lump of coal in the man's chest, he still expected that Marcus would eventually come around and marry someone from their social circle—preferably someone Jewish, but at the very least someone who came from money. A woman to give birth to an heir who could be molded in the Rosemann image.

In the pause between when he dropped the bomb and his aunts commenced the freak-out he knew would come, he snuck a glance at Rose. Other than the fact that her eyes had turned into saucers, he had to give her major props for playing it cool.

"Marcus," Cary drawled, clearly not buying the charade. "Why didn't you *tell* us?" Cary knew him better than anyone, so Marcus could only hope that even if he hadn't fooled his cousin, everyone else was buying the story.

"It just happened a couple days ago," he said, compounding the lie as Rose started coughing.

"At last, the succession is assured!" said Cary. Then he winked at Rose and said, "I'm as gay as the day is long, so Marcus here was our only hope. But no pressure or anything."

"This evening is not about Marcus," said Mr. Rosemann, as if Marcus had somehow been trying to steal the limelight. He might hate his father, but Marcus would never stoop so low as to cause any trouble at his mother's beloved Fall Ball.

Undeterred and clearly enjoying Marcus's discomfort, Cary asked, "When is the wedding?"

Aunt Ruth followed with, "Will it be a Jewish wedding?"

"You'll have to convert, Rose," said Rachel, who was never one for beating around the bush. "Otherwise the children won't be Jewish."

"But look how handy it is that she has an "R" name!" Cary said with false joviality, interrupting Rose's attempt to respond. "She'll fit right in!"

"Enough." Marcus raised his voice to let them all know he was serious. Everyone stopped talking and turned to look at him, except his father, who merely stared at his plate. He could feel his father's interest in the conversation, though. It was the same nonchalant attention he paid to Marcus's report cards and to his at-bats in Little League. Bart Rose-mann was not a warm man. Yet he cared very deeply about the outcomes of report cards and at-bats—and the breeding or lack thereof of his only son's intended bride. The rub, of course, was that he didn't actually care about whether Marcus liked baseball, who his friends were at school, or if Marcus's wife-to-be made Marcus happy. He was concerned only with the outcome. The outcome must always be correct, no matter the path required to get there. "Give us a break," Marcus said, summoning a fake smile. "We haven't made any decisions yet."

"Oh, we might as well just tell them, Marcus," said Rose, apparently no longer content to remain silent. He had a mere moment to think that the situation was about to spin out of control before she burst out with, "I can't have kids, actually."

He didn't know whether to wish that the earth would open up and swallow them or to stand and applaud. If his goal had been to aggravate his father, his "fiancée" had just turned the dial up to eleven.

"So really, there's no point in me converting, I'm thinking." Rose cocked her head as if considering a puzzle. Then she smiled with a brightness he recognized as artificial. "Oh, look, here's my vegetarian dinner. Yum. No dead animals for me!"

She proceeded to tuck into a plate of very dull-looking

fettuccini alfredo, apparently oblivious to the dropped jaws around the table.

Damn. The thing about Rose, Marcus was learning, was that you never knew what you were going to get with her. That was not a feeling he was accustomed to. Generally, he commanded, and he received. The world conformed to his expectations. But Rose. She was like some kind of goddess on a mountain, throwing down random thunderbolts to mess with the mere mortals below her. From manipulating him into making that donation to EcoHabitat to her vehement revulsion when he'd shown her the Magnifique mockups to upping the ante so dramatically on their little charade just now, she was completely unpredictable.

It was unsettling.

She was unsettling.

Especially when she was stomping on his foot with her spiked heel. "Ow!" he muttered. What was it with this woman? Earlier—both yesterday on the phone and before dinner at the bar—she had him telling her his whole life story. And now she was *stamping on his foot*? Had he fallen into an alternate dimension?

Another stomp. "Rose, sweetie," he said, turning toward her and suddenly getting that whole Shakespeare thing about daggers in men's smiles. She was smiling, but she also managed to look like she wanted to murder him. "Didn't you say you wanted to use the powder room before the salad course?" Without waiting for a response, he pulled out her chair for her, forcing her to stand. She stumbled a little, but he caught her.

"Yes. Thank you for reminding me, *poopsie*."

"After you," he ground out, waiting to make sure she

was actually going to obey him.

He was a little mesmerized as she did so, watching her hips sway in that blue and silver striped dress that made her look like a jewel in an ash heap. She led them out of the ballroom and into a small alcove in the hotel lobby. Then she whirled, hands on hips. "Mar-cus."

Oh, she was not pleased. He could tell from the way she over-enunciated his name.

"Mar-cus."

There it was again. But this time, her voice was quieter, and she drew out the two syllables of his name on a sigh. Objectively, he knew she was angry, but the breathy, low quality of her voice brought to mind something else. It went straight to his cock, truth be told. For a moment, he could imagine she was saying his name in something other than anger.

She poked him in the chest. "What *the actual* fuck?"

Okay, no, who was he kidding? It was anger.

"You just told your family we were *engaged*."

"And you just told them you were barren!"

"You started it! And who uses the word *barren* anymore, Marcus?" she yelled. "Last time I checked, it was no longer the nineteenth century."

He glanced around. The few people in the lobby were definitely paying attention to their spat. He'd wanted inappropriate, yes, but he didn't want to ruin his mother's Fall Ball. It was a fine line. She took a step closer to him and poked again. People didn't just *poke* him. He grabbed her hand.

"What kind of bullshit, privileged world do you live in?" she went on, her rant gathering steam. She tried to pull her hand from his, but no way was he letting her go. "Your family was looking at me like I was a racehorse they were thinking of buying. It's—"

He pulled her flush against him, crushing her breasts against his chest. Lowering his head to the side of her neck, he got a whiff of that maddeningly sexy herbal scent of hers. He dragged his face up the side of her neck. When his lips reached her ear, she shivered noticeably. "Everyone is watching your little tantrum," he whispered. "If you don't stop yelling, I'm going to kiss you so hard, it will make you shut up."

She stopped yelling.

He was a little disappointed, truth be told.

They stayed like that for a long moment, like wild animals in a standoff. She clung to him, breathing heavily. He hated to extend the horse metaphor, but she reminded him right now of a spooked horse. A soft, curvy, warm spooked horse.

Slowly, slowly, he backed away, maintaining eye contact with her the whole way.

Their deadlock continued as they stared at each other. It was strange how many times in the past few days he had found himself in a stalemate with Rose, staring intensely at her as she refused to back down.

Then, suddenly, she burst out laughing.

What the hell?

If there was one way Rose could have gained the upper hand in their battle of wills just now, it could only have been by *laughing*. He'd been right earlier: Rose *never* did what you expected her to. But as she laughed, it was as if all the tension dissipated from the air around them. She moved to sit on a nearby sofa and slumped against its back as she sighed theatrically. She'd done that in the cab the other day, too, and he was beginning to recognize it as a signature move. "Well, that was weird," she said.

He lowered himself to sit beside her, still a little disconcerted by how quickly the tenor of their encounter had changed.

She looked thoughtful. "Don't take this the wrong way, but your father is an asshole. I had thought you must be exaggerating, but no. It's like he has some kind of special brand of disdain he reserves just for you."

Cary was always telling him he was being overly sensitive when he complained about just that. It was like he just refused to see it. Everyone in his family just accepted his father's God-given right to be a brute. "You got that from being in there?"

"Are you kidding me? It's like he's the Snow Queen. He practically breathes ice crystals when he talks to you. Why do you think he's like that?"

"I think it's just his nature. As long as I can remember, he's been riding my ass."

"You have no siblings?" she asked.

"No. Cary is like a little brother, though. He lived next door to us growing up, and he and I are both only children."

"Your father mentioned that he was separated from your mother prior to her death."

"Yeah. He was in the process of divorcing her." There was that familiar surge of rage that always came over him when he thought of his parents' breakup. Or, to phrase it more accurately, when he thought of his father breaking his mother's heart, throwing her away after she'd been nothing but devoted to him for four decades.

"If your parents were estranged, why is he here?" she

asked. "Why is he involved in the Fall Ball—or anything at all?" She nodded at the ballroom. "Everyone in there is from her side of the family, yes?"

Marcus sighed. "It's so weirdly complicated that I don't know if I have an answer that makes sense. To begin with, Ruth's son Cary—you met him—is his second in command at the investment firm."

"That's awkward."

"You'd think," Marcus agreed. "But it's like they bracket the work stuff from the family stuff."

"Wouldn't it be even easier to bracket it if your father wasn't part of the family stuff? And if he was divorcing your mother—against her wishes, it sounds like—I can't imagine why her sisters continue to put up with him."

"It's worse than that." Marcus turned to look at her. He never talked about his family, but now that he'd started, he couldn't seem to stop. "He started divorce proceedings because she caught him with his mistress. She'd known about the affair—it was a longstanding one. We all knew. We just never talked about it. But somehow being caught—having his two worlds intersect—enraged him. My mother tried to calm him. She wanted to stay married, if you can believe it. But he wasn't having it. It was like the train had left the station, and there was nothing she could do about it."

"And then she got sick, and even that didn't stop him," Rose finished, having got a perfect read on his father.

He laughed, but there was no mirth in it. "Yes. I do take a sick sort of pleasure in the fact that she died before the divorce was final."

"So why does he stick around if he wanted out of his marriage so badly?"

"To torture us?" Marcus asked the ceiling. When Rosie made a disbelieving noise, he said, "I don't know how to explain it. My father is really big on family, despite the fact that his actions would suggest otherwise."

"He's big on the *concept* of family, maybe, rather than the well-being of his actual family." Again, she had sized up the situation perfectly, named it in a way he hadn't been able to.

"You and your mother were close?" she asked, her tone gentle.

It was hard to explain. It wasn't like he and his mother had been chummy. They hadn't played tennis together or even talked that much on a day-to-day basis. But she had always been a quiet, strong presence, whispering in his ear that she loved him. That he could do anything. Be anything. He didn't know how to sum up all that, so he settled for just saying, "Yes."

"You know what you should do if you really want to bug your father? You should *actually marry* someone totally in-appropriate. Not me, mind you. You can find someone worse than me. I'm just your garden variety agnostic, but I could set you up with a nice Hindu girl. Or—oh!—a nice Hindu boy!" She laughed. "I can ask my mother to find two of them for us! Then you and Cary could both be hopeless on the whole 'producing an heir' front."

She was kidding, but he couldn't stop himself from saying, "Nope. I don't do relationships."

She stopped laughing and cocked her head at him. "So you've said."

"I don't think I got that gene. I blame my father," he said, wanting to make her go back to laughing—laughing suited her so well. It didn't work.

"Well, it's probably for the best," she said, which was a surprise. He would have expected her to give him some kind of bullshit "true love conquers all" pep talk. She jerked her head toward the ballroom. "Pity the poor woman who has to do that for real."

"You aren't wrong." The only woman who could probably stand it was one who'd grown up in what Rose called that "bullshit, privileged" world and thought of it as normal.

"You have to give me some props, though," she continued. "I gave it my best shot in there." He dipped his head in acknowledgment. "But as much as I'm sympathetic to this campaign of aggravation you're waging against your villainous father, I can't be your fake fiancée."

He was about to concede, but, suddenly, an idea was forming. A wicked idea. "Why can't you?" he asked, turning sideways on the sofa so he was facing her. "I mean, really? Why not?"

"Because it's ridiculous."

"Don't take this the wrong way, but we don't exactly run in the same circles."

"I think we've established that, and thank God for it," she said. "Your circles are exhausting."

"My point is that if you pretended to be my fiancée for, say, a month—"

"No. You're asking me to be your human Barbie doll. You would pose me how you wanted to get maximum mileage out of my *unsuitability*." She wrinkled her nose. "No thanks."

She was right. It was a presumptuous thing to ask. He massaged his temples—his head was beginning to ache.

"You're right. Forget it." He summoned a smile, which probably looked as fake as it felt. "Thanks for playing along as much as you did. You really stuck it to my father in there." He stuck out his hand. "It was nice knowing you, Rose Verma."

"Wait." Her eyes darted around in confusion. "What are you going to do?"

He shrugged. "I'm going to go in there and tell them I made it up." He smiled at her astonished reaction. Something about her made him want to confess. "No. That's a lie. I'm going to go in there and tell them we broke up."

"Just now. Out here."

"Don't worry. I'll tell them *you* dumped *me*." He stood. "Maybe I'll tell them that you dumped me because of what a charming family I have."

"Whoa, whoa, whoa. Hang on." She grabbed his sleeve and tugged hard enough that he sat back down.

Her eyes narrowed. "Let's just say, for the sake of argument, that I agreed to this harebrained scheme. What's in it for me?"

"You mean besides the existential satisfaction of helping me aggravate my despicable father beyond belief?" He couldn't help teasing her. She was too easy a target, and their lighthearted banter was a relief after the heaviness of recounting the story of his fucked up family.

"Yes. Beyond that."

"You want another donation for the birdies?"

Her chin rose. "I do indeed."

He tried not to laugh—they were bargaining, after all. But sparring with Rose was so satisfying. "I'll do you one better. I'll save the birdies, *and* I'll redo EcoHabitat's shit website."

"Our website is not shit." There was a slight pause, then she shook her head and blew out a breath. "Oh, what am I saying? I'm trying to be all loyal, but of course our website is shit. It's a complete disaster."

"So let me redo it."

"What do you mean by redo?" she asked.

"Total overhaul. New architecture, new content as needed, new navigation, new design." He could see that he'd interested her.

"You can do all that yourself, Mr. CEO?"

Why did it sting that she looked so surprised? "Most of it. Some of the programming and content development I'll outsource. But I'll supervise everything closely."

She chewed on her lip. Why was she looking so unenthused? Did she not understand that he was offering tens of thousands of dollars' worth of pro-bono services? "What's the problem?"

"No problem. I'm just thinking about how to...stage this."

"What do you mean?" he asked.

"Mr. Carroll won't approve. I've been pitching him on the idea of a new website, and he's just not down with it."

"Tony Carroll reports to the board of directors, does he not?"

She nodded, eyeing him with suspicion. "Yes."

"So you do a power play," he said. "Present some of the board members with the finished product. They'd have to be idiots not to see it as an improvement. Then you present Tony with a *fait accompli*."

"Right, but you're forgetting the part where we're not

all-powerful one-percenters." Rose poked him *again* as she spoke. But it was more of a friendly poke this time, so he let it stand. "In my world, the fundraising manager can't just show up for tea at a board member's house and say 'Hi, you want to hear about this idea I have?'"

"Ah," he said, delivering the final parry. "You're forgetting that *I* can. My mother was friends with all these people." And if that didn't work, Marcus would just make an enormous donation and start throwing his weight around as a major donor and son of the charity's late guardian angel. But he wouldn't tell Rose that just now. She wasn't the kind of woman who would want him to charge in and start using his authority to solve her problems.

She cocked her head. She wanted the new website—he could almost feel the yearning radiating off her. "And you would do this all? Just to get me to participate in this crackpot scheme, the sole point of which is to bother your father?"

God, when she said it like that it sounded so...petty. Still, he believed in owning one's actions, so he merely gazed directly at her and said, "That is correct."

"I'm not going to, like, be at your side constantly."

He had to suppress the urge to fist pump. He had hooked her. "How about this? Hanukkah starts about three weeks from now. We have a big family dinner on the first night. Come with me, and then we'll break up afterward. So it's not even a month of your time."

"I don't have to do anything else between now and then?"

"Not unless you want to." He licked his lips. He thought she could take the joke. "Being engaged could come with certain benefits." God, listen to him. It's like he was proposing a type of friends-with-benefits arrangement. Fake-fiancés-with-benefits? Rose, the bleeding heart vegetarian who looked like she was visiting from Oz wasn't his usual type — that had been the whole point — but, damn. He was surprised by how much the idea of her underneath him turned him on.

She either missed or chose to ignore the insinuation. Probably the former because she was gazing off into space, lost in her thoughts. He took the opportunity to admire her from afar. Her light brown skin positively glowed in the warm light of the lobby, and her hair, which she'd poufed up somehow for the occasion, looked messy-on-purpose, a disheveled black waterfall. It was a good look on her. What a dick his father was. And TallDoctor, too, for that matter. How could anyone look at Rose and find her lacking?

She finally turned to look at him. "If I agree to play this stupid game, I'm not going to stop my Thursday night dates."

Like hell she wasn't. "You can't date other people when you're fake-engaged to me, Rose."

"I'm not getting any younger. I'm still on a schedule."

"Not happening."

"You just said yourself that we don't run in the same social circles," she argued. "No one you know is ever going to know if I go on three dates between now and Hanukkah."

He blinked. He honestly hadn't been thinking about the idea of someone discovering her on a date. It was more that the idea of other guys out with his fake fiancée…it rankled. But the key word there was *fake*, wasn't it? He didn't like it, but he couldn't credibly tell her what to do. He sighed. "Fine. Go on your dates."

She stuck out her hand. "All right, then. Make another donation, redo my website, and get me an audience with a board member or two, and you've got yourself a fake fiancée."

He was supposed to shake her hand. But he wanted to rattle her. He wanted her to remember him when she was on her Thursday night dates. So he brought her hand to his lips and kissed it, letting his open mouth drag across the back of her hand. When she didn't pull away—in fact, she inhaled sharply—he turned her hand over and did the same thing to her palm.

There. Take that, Rose Verma.

Chapter Five

Rosie was feeling a little bit like Cinderella after the ball. It was embarrassing, really, but she couldn't stop humming as she made breakfast and paged through the newspaper. If there had been any woodland creatures in her apartment, they would have circled around her and sung a song.

After they'd finished their weird negotiation—why did all her interactions with Marcus end up with them striking some kind of bargain?—they'd gone back into the ballroom. She'd expected everything to be tense and formal and stuffy. And it kind of was as they finished dinner, with his relatives making polite but forced-sounding chitchat while his father sat in utter silence.

But once the dancing started and they were untethered from their table, the evening had taken a...compelling turn. It was a rare guy who would get up and dance without requiring any cajoling or plying with alcohol or requesting of some stupid frat boy "bro" song from the DJ. It was an even rarer guy who suggested dancing himself. So when Marcus turned to her and whispered, "What do you say we hit the dance floor and burn off some of this Rosemann family tension?" she'd had to restrain herself from doing a little pre-dancing dance of joy.

But then, oh but then. She had melted into his arms as if she belonged there. That commandeering personality of his was extremely effective on the dance floor. When he wasn't telling her what to do with words, somehow she could relax into the sensation of him telling her what to do with his body as he moved them around. But, strangely, though she was undeniably aroused by his proximity, she wasn't flustered, as she so often was on her Thursday night dates. Maybe it was the fact that with Marcus, there was no pressure. He had outright told her that he didn't do relationships, so even if he had been her type—which he wasn't—he wasn't boyfriend material. Not having to worry about the impression she was making was amazingly freeing. She just needed to keep everything in perspective. Because being at ease with *and* crazy-attracted to Marcus could get dangerous.

The phone rang.

"Rosie!" It was Hailey, breathless. "Have you seen *Gossip TO* this morning?"

"What do you think?" It wasn't that she was above celebrity gossip, but she only cared about celebrities she'd actually heard of. B-list Canadian TV stars and Toronto socialites that were generally featured in *Gossip TO* didn't make the cut. Hailey, on the other hand, was trying to expand her freelance makeup artist business, so she monitored the local party scene with great interest.

"I think you should have a look right now."

Rosie fired up her laptop. Hailey probably wanted to analyze someone's makeup. And given that Rosie was the recipient of a free weekly makeover, the least she could do was— "Oh my God."

"Told ya."

Her hands began to shake so hard that she had to put down the coffee cup she'd been holding.

"At least you look good," Hailey said. "You look *really* good for paparazzi shots. What I want to know is are you going to change your name? Because I can't decide if Rose Rosemann is the worst name ever or a genius move."

"It's not true!" she wailed. *It's only fake-true!*

"It's gossip," Hailey said. "It doesn't have to be true."

"I'll call you back," said Rosie, hanging up over the sounds of Hailey's protest.

Hailey was right that the photos weren't bad. There were three of them. They were all from after dinner. The first showed Marcus embracing her outside the ballroom, after their fight. From this angle, with his head buried in her neck, he looked like he wanted to...devour her. It must be true what they say about love and hate being two sides of the same coin, because although Rosie knew they had been bitterly arguing, they basically looked like they couldn't keep their hands off each other.

The second shot was of him kissing her hand. Her face got hot just thinking about it. Who knew a hand kiss could be so powerful?

The final photo was of Marcus helping her into the car as she smiled at him like a simple-minded fool. She tried to imagine any of her Thursday night dates doing that. Marcus could be a jerk, but he had a chivalrous streak. She thought also of the flowers he'd brought her and the hand kiss in the previous photo. There was an old-fashioned courtliness about him, but it was overlain with power. It was a potent combination.

But all that was beside the point. Time to stop staring at herself on the screen and face the fact that she had a big-ass problem.

"Well, hello there, pseudo-wife-to-be." Marcus couldn't help but smile as he answered Rose's call. After their spat immediately following his surprise announcement last night, she had proven surprisingly good-natured about the whole charade. So much so that it had turned out to be a fun evening, which was not at all what he had expected. The Fall Ball was never what he would call fun. It was a family obligation he endured. And the first Fall Ball without his mother? He'd banked on it being excruciating. But it turned out Rose could really bust a move. Not to mention turn heads. A bunch of men—including him—had trouble keeping their eyes off her. Which suited his purposes entirely in terms of flaunting her in front of his father, even if it had made him want to start a brawl or two with some of the more egregious oglers.

All in all, though, he was considering it a stroke of luck that she was being so cool about this whole thing.

"Marcus!" she shouted. "You have ruined my life!"

Well. So much for cool. "You'll have to be a little more specific."

"Have you seen *Gossip TO* this morning?"

"I don't even know what you're talking about."

"It's a website about local society happenings."

He grabbed his iPad, which he'd been using to read the papers over breakfast. "Give me the URL, and I'll have a look."

"Huh," he said, taking in the pictures and reading the accompanying text.

LOCAL AD-MAN MARCUS ROSEMANN OF THE OLD-MONEY TORONTO ROSEMANNS ANNOUNCED HIS ENGAGEMENT LAST NIGHT AT THE CLAN'S ANNUAL CHARITY BALL. THE LUCKY BRIDE-TO-BE IS ROSE VERMA, ABOUT WHOM NOT MUCH IS KNOWN (BUT KILLER DRESS, *NON*, EVEN IF IT WAS A BIT RISQUÉ FOR THAT PARTICULAR SOIREE?). OUR SOURCES SAY THE ROSEMANNS ARE NOT PLEASED. MARCUS HAS ALWAYS BEEN A BIT OF A LONE WOLF, THOUGH, *NON*?

He set down the iPad. A part of him understood that this was serious, but he had to stifle a laugh. "That *was* a killer dress."

"Why am I the *lucky bride*?" said Rose, voice dripping with scorn. "Why aren't you the lucky groom?"

"A fair question. Anyone who looks at these pictures can see who the catch is in this fake relationship." He meant it. Rose looked absolutely stunning in the pictures. Her obvious beauty aside, the joy in her face was infectious—especially in the shot where he was helping her into the car. Even he was grinning like an idiot in that one. And Marcus was pretty sure that in the twenty years of its existence, he had never—not even once—grinned at the Fall Ball.

"What are we going to do?" she wailed. "People can *not* think I'm engaged. If anything, I need to step *up* the dating game. I'm running out of time!"

"When exactly is the big three-oh?"

"January twenty-third."

"And, what?" he asked. "Your mother is going to literally have you married off that day if you're still single?" He was having trouble imagining anyone making Rose do something she didn't want to.

Rose huffed a bitter laugh. "You don't know my mother. And you'd better hope it stays that way because if she finds out about us, you will rue the day you decided to get fake-engaged to me."

"She won't like me?"

"Unclear. But I guarantee she will not leave you alone. She'll probably move into your house in an attempt to assess your suitability for me. If she doesn't get to pick out my boyfriend, she's going to be *all over* the poor bastard I nominate for the job."

He chuckled. "She wants you to marry an Indian guy?"

"Sort of." She sighed. "It's complicated."

"Try me. We Rosemanns are masters of complicated. And you heard my whole sordid family history last night."

"We were at my cousin's wedding," she explained. "He married this great girl—they were so happy. That's where it all started—and, really, she meddles because she wants me to be happy. I don't think she cares inherently what kind of person I marry. It's more that she thinks I'd have more in common with an Indian man, or at least a south Asian. And I know she thinks my previous relationship problems were at least partially due to culture clash, which is ridiculous because I was a child when I came here—this *is* my culture."

"In some ways, it's not that different than my family," he said. "My aunt Rachel aside, no one really practices Judaism in any meaningful way. But they all think there's this cultural shorthand that matters."

"Maybe it does," she said thoughtfully.

We're Jewish because we're Jewish, his father always said. *And what you are means something.* "I think it can if you want it to, but I don't think it *has* to be a barrier," he said, surprised to find himself thinking seriously about the matter—about Rose and her dating dilemmas. "And unlike in my family, your mother probably genuinely wants what's best for you."

"You're right about that. She's reacting, at least in part, to my childhood. We lived in Aurora, which was the middle of nowhere back then. I was the only non-white kid in my grade." Her voice had grown wistful. "I could seriously have used a friend from my so-called culture. Well, actually, who am I kidding? I could have used a friend from any culture for a couple years there."

"You were a loner, it sounds like?"

"Not by choice." She huffed a laugh. "But after my best friend moved away, it took me some time to find my feet. And I was this tall back then, so that didn't help."

The idea of Rose being lonely didn't sit well with him. He wanted to ask more, but she kept talking.

"The point is, part of me wouldn't be surprised to end up content with some random guy my mom sets me up with through her network."

"And the other part?"

"The other part says contentment is not enough, and so

I am on a mission. There are only seven Thursday nights left before my birthday, Marcus!"

"Why only go out once a week if you're really so determined?" he asked, genuinely curious. He wasn't usually a chatter, but there was something about talking on the phone with Rose that made him feel less wound up than usual.

"I may have to up the frequency in the final stretch here." She paused. "You didn't see it, but I just shuddered. At the moment, I only date once a week because it's pretty much all I can handle. I usually need a week to recover."

"And why Thursdays in particular?" he asked, still finding himself displeased with the idea of her going on all those dates.

"Because a weekend night sends a message that things are serious," she declared. "You can't send that message so early on in a relationship."

"All these rules."

"You don't even know."

"It sounds tiring."

"It's not only that," said Rose, talking faster as if warming to the topic. "It's also the fact that you don't want to ruin the weekend with a bad date. Sometimes, the only way I can get over it enough to sleep is to write to my best friend about it—the letter you got by mistake was one of those. So I do my Thursday night date, write my Thursday night letter, and then the weekend is logistically *and* emotionally clear."

"You have this down to a science," he teased.

"I do—by necessity. But we're getting off topic." She was right. He'd forgotten that she called him about the gossip site. "The point is, I can't let this fake engagement get in the way of my real dating." She laughed. "Now there's a sentence

I never thought I'd hear myself say."

"Well, you might just have to give up the dating." He lowered his voice. "I'll make it worth your while."

"What can you do beyond the website?"

He hadn't been thinking of the website, but there was no way he could say that since she'd missed his innuendo. He wasn't used to that. The women he spent time with never missed innuendos. He sighed, at war with himself, but ultimately knowing that he couldn't ask Rose to jeopardize Operation: Boyfriend for him. "Look at it this way. If any of your Mr. Thursday Nights have seen *Gossip TO* and remember you from it, that's probably a sign that you should weed them out, no? Do you really want to date a grown man who reads gossip websites?"

"You're right, of course. But my larger question is, is this going to get out there? Really out there? Given that you're apparently some kind of famous person."

He paused, trying to think how to explain it. "Have you ever seen the show *Gossip Girl*?"

"Oh my God. Are you trying to say you're Chuck Bass?"

He laughed in spite of himself. "My best friend Lauren was consumed with that show when it came out. She made me watch the first season with her."

"This Lauren seems like kind of a weird best friend for you. You don't seem like the *Gossip Girl* type *at all*."

It probably did look weird from the outside. "We go way back," he said by way of explanation.

"You dated?"

"God, no." Lauren would have laughed so hard to hear Rose ask that. "She's a lesbian."

"Marcus, you have hidden depths."

He smiled. In the strange, cozy alternate-reality that was talking on the phone with Rose, he was pleased to be thought of as a person with hidden depths. "Anyway, she's my executive creative director at the agency, and she's pop culture obsessed, which is useful in our line of work. My point is that although the world of *Gossip Girl* was an extreme example, I do come from a similar sort of scene. Rich people can get fixated on stupid things. So while I'm far from *famous*, to use your term, my family is known in certain circles."

"So this engagement will be a big thing now that it's out?"

"Not necessarily. But some of my family's social circle will probably hear about it. But you know what? I think things have gone far enough. I never meant to cause you any trouble. Let's just call it off. We annoyed my father enormously, I think—especially if his friends have heard about the engagement—so mission accomplished."

Rose sighed theatrically. "It's okay. Hanukkah isn't that far away, really. Buuuut…" She drew out the word.

"What?"

"There is one more thing you can do for me to express your gratitude."

"More money for the birdies?" he teased.

"I need someone to babysit Fifi on Thursday night."

"No." There was no reality alternate enough for him to agree to dog-sit.

"It turns out she gets very nervous if she's left alone for a long stretch. She actually destroyed my apartment the night of the Fall Ball. I have a neighbor looking in on her over lunch, and that seems to have calmed her enough to be cool until I get home, but if I'm gone all day *and* all evening, she loses her mind. I was going to have to hire a dog-sitter for date night."

"I don't know why you're telling me all this."

"I'm telling you this because I'm *reaaaally* looking forward to Hanukkah," she drawled. "I've never been to a Hanukkah dinner."

He groaned, and she must have taken it for assent, because her voice brightened considerably as she said, "Thanks! You're the best fake fiancé ever! I'll drop a key and instructions at your office on Thursday."

Then she hung up.

Sometime—not now, but sometime—he was going to have to examine what it meant that not only was he shoveling money at a cause he was indifferent to and designing a website pro bono, he was now signed up to babysit a destructive beagle named Fifi. All in the name of irritating his father.

That was probably a little screwed up.

Waiting for the elevator to Marcus's office in the Lakeview Centre, Rosie started to think that maybe she was in over her head.

"Holy crap," said Hailey, who had accompanied Rosie on the lunchtime errand, despite the fact that Rosie had assured her there was no chance they would see Marcus. He was head of the company, after all, and she was just planning to drop an envelope for him at reception.

"This is some serious commerce going down here," Hailey added, looking around with undisguised fascination at the lunchtime crowds streaming on and off the elevators. Of course, Hailey stood out with her hair—currently purple— and her Sex Pistols shirt, but Rosie, in her normal office clothes, did too. Nearly everyone who belonged in the building was dressed in suits, be they men or women. The odd dress in a real color stood out, but Rosie feared she *really* stood out in her too-casual black and white polka-dotted skirt and drapey pink top. It was just like junior high, or that damned Fall Ball—she never got it right. The funny thing was she'd gotten a little extra dressed up today *because* she was coming here. Which was stupid because she had already established in her mind that she wasn't going to see Marcus on this trip, and what did she care what his receptionist thought of her? Still, her outfit, in contrast to all these conservative suits, made her feel like a twelve-year-old at take-your-kids-to-work day.

Her discomfort only intensified as they crowded onto the elevator. Staring at the numbers above the door as they silently ascended, she could feel the eyes of one person in particular on her. She snuck a glance to the side. Sure enough, a woman was looking at her, pretty openly, too. With short blonde hair and a purple felt dress over a crisp white shirt, the woman was the only person on board who didn't have the "finance drone" look. She seemed very stylish and sophisticated.

And she got off at the forty-ninth floor along with Rosie and Hailey. Of course.

Well, there was nothing to do but own it and just continue with her errand. It wasn't like there was anything illegal about being underdressed in an office building. She snuck a glance at Hailey. Or having purple hair in an office building.

The reception area looked just like these things always did in the movies. The desk might as well have been a fortress. Sleek and rounded, it made her feel as if she were a serf approaching the drawbridge of the local castle.

"May I help you?"

The desk was on a platform, so the fact that even Rosie had to look up to meet the receptionist's eyes only reinforced the whole medieval vibe.

She cleared her throat. "Yes. May I leave this for Marcus Rosemann, please? He's expecting it."

"Oh my God," said the receptionist. "You're—"

"Rose," said the stylish woman from the elevator. She stuck out her hand. "I'm Lauren Daelin, creative director at the Rosemann Agency."

Oh! This was the best friend. She shook the woman's hand and stumbled through introducing Hailey.

"Let me take you to Marcus. He's free now, and he won't want to miss you."

"Oh, no!" she said, probably a tad too vehemently because the receptionist's brows furrowed. "I don't want to interrupt his work. We agreed that I would just drop this off." Neither woman made a move to take the envelope. "He's taking care of my dog tonight," she added weakly, as if more detail would make her sound *less* lame.

"Is he now?" Lauren's eyes narrowed, not unkindly, but as if she was trying to piece together a great mystery.

A buzzing sound prompted the receptionist to pick up a phone.

"That'll be Marcus looking for me," said Lauren. "We have a meeting."

"Yes," said the receptionist into the receiver. "She's right here with your…Rose. Yes, sir. I will." The woman set the phone down and looked at Rosie. "He says to wait here, and he'll be out in a second." Then she turned to Lauren. "And he says to ask you if you guys can meet at two instead of now."

"We can indeed," Lauren said, eyes twinkling.

Clearly, these women knew who she was. The question was did they *really* know? Had they read the gossip site and therefore thought she was truly Marcus's fiancée? Or had he disavowed her at the office and everyone was in on the game? She wasn't sure which option she preferred.

"Rose," he said, and she jumped, which was stupid because she'd known he was on his way. But she'd expected him to emerge from the door behind the reception desk. Instead, he'd snuck up on them from behind, where there was an unmarked mahogany door she hadn't noticed.

She had never seen him in his office persona. He looked different than he had at the ball. More formal, which should have been impossible, since the ball had been black tie. But he was all tricked out in a conservative gray suit and a black and white herringbone-patterned silk tie that probably cost more than her whole outfit. He should have looked like one of the drones she'd seen getting on and off the elevators in the lobby, but for some reason he did not.

Noooo, he did not.

Because *formal* wasn't the only word she would use to describe him. As he strode across the reception area toward them, he was also…uncontained. As if the suit was not sufficient to mask the powerful limbs that lay beneath it. There was a kind of casual, entitled dominance about him in this environment. The receptionist sat up straighter, as if to demonstrate the point.

"Hi there," said Marcus, sticking out his hand in front of Hailey. "We met the other day, but not really. I'm Marcus Rosemann."

"Hailey Chang," said Rosie's friend weakly. And Hailey was never weak. What was the *deal* with this guy? He seemed a far cry from the man she'd had a surprisingly intimate phone call with the other night.

"Rose tells me you're a makeup artist," he said.

"That's right."

"We're bidding on a big project for Magnifique. You know the brand?"

Hailey nodded. "A solid brand, if a bit stuffy."

Marcus looked at Lauren and said, "Exactly." Then he turned his attention back to them. "Hailey, would you be amenable to a little five-minute focus group? We'd love to get an expert opinion. Can you show her some of the sketches, Lauren?" Hailey looked at Rosie, as if seeking permission. But before Rosie could say anything—something like *don't abandon me*, perhaps? Or *Magnifique tortures baby bunnies*—Marcus added, "And then maybe you can take Lauren's card and send over some clips at your convenience. We do a lot of shoots and can always use another good makeup artist in the Rolodex."

Smooth, Rosie thought as Lauren led her friend away. He must really want Hailey's input because he had to have known that he'd just dangled a dream gig in front of the makeup artist.

"Now you're mine." The whisper in her ear shot straight down her spine.

Or maybe he had some other ulterior motive. She

started to sweat, despite the fact that the office was ultra air-conditioned.

"Come with me," he said.

"Everything is right here," she countered, extending the envelope toward him. "Keys, instructions…"

He hitched his head in the direction from which he'd come. "Let's go."

And God help her, she followed him. She was starting to understand that Marcus was the kind of man people obeyed. It was probably why he was so good at advertising. They were likely going to his office, but for all she knew, they were headed to the seventh circle of hell, and she was just dumbly trailing along behind him.

The door opened onto a space that was home to a small cluster of cubicles. But they were the fanciest cubicles Rosie had ever seen—made out of some kind of dark wood, they were a far cry from their cousins at EcoHabitat. The space had been filled with the hum of activity. But as they made their way through it, chatter died and heads turned. It was like Marcus was the bad-guy emperor from *Star Wars* or something. If they'd been walking through a forest, all the "birdies" he had been cutting checks for would have fallen silent.

But he strode through it all unmoved, as if it were normal for people to be struck dumb at the sight of him. She breathed a sigh of relief when they turned a corner and emerged into a lushly carpeted area. He led her past another, smaller reception desk occupied by a woman who looked to be about sixty.

"No interruptions for the next little while, Carla."

"Yes, sir."

"Your assistant calls you *sir*?" she couldn't help but scoff after he closed the door behind them. But the thought was soon replaced by another, namely, "Whoa. Nice digs."

"Yeah, well, I spend more time here than I do at home."

The office was gorgeous. A large art-deco desk dominated one end. The other featured a sitting area with a sofa upholstered in a muted silvery-gray brushed velvet. The colors were subdued, like his gray suit. But also like the suit, the space conveyed a slight edge. A sense that something more than met the eye might be lurking below the surface. Though her personal tastes ran toward more vibrant colors, the textures of the office called to her. She wanted so badly to go over to that sofa and run her hand over it.

It was as if he'd heard her silent wish because he gestured her over. She tried to be subtle about rubbing her bare forearms over the fabric—which did not disappoint—as she sat. "So what's up? Did you bring me here just to impress me with your swish office?" She glanced out the wall of windows, which featured a stunning skyline view. "Because it's totally working."

He tore open the envelope. "I just want to make sure I understand everything."

"It's not hard. Keys, leash on a hook by the door, two scoops of food, which is under the sink, after you get back from walking her."

He was examining the written instructions she'd included in the package. "I take my responsibility to Fifi extremely seriously. What time will you be home?"

"Do I have a curfew?" She'd been going for a teasing note, but the question came out sounding kind of peevish, as if this really was take-your-kids-to-work day.

"It doesn't matter. I'm a night owl. And I'm going to work on your site, so I'll have plenty to do. Who holds the title Mr. Thursday Night tonight?"

"Anderson361."

He looked at her for a moment and scowled. She thought he was going to say something mean, but then he surprised her. "That's kind of funny."

"Is it? I couldn't decide if it was funny or lame."

"It's funny if his name is Anderson. It's *really* funny if he's actually Anderson Cooper." He smirked. "But then I guess you'd be barking up the wrong tree."

"His last name is Anderson," she said. "Chad Anderson."

"And what do you know about Mr. Anderson?"

"He's a management consultant." She paused. "That's one of those jobs where I don't actually know what it means." She pulled out her phone and pulled up his picture. "He's cute, though."

Marcus took the phone from her and cocked his head as he examined Chad. "He looks like he's seventeen."

"Yeah, he is a bit younger than I am, but…" Rosie trailed off when Marcus gave her the phone back. Alrighty then. Apparently Chad had been dismissed.

"I can't get to your place until six or six thirty. Is that okay?"

"Totally fine. And make yourself at home. Not to be too much of an ethnic stereotype, but there is some pretty amazing curry in the fridge. It's from my mom." She meant it, but suddenly, the thought of Marcus in her house, his tie loosened, eating her food…it was unsettling. She cleared her throat. "This is the part where I would say thank you, but I still think you owe me way more than I owe you. Does everyone in your company know about me?"

"Apparently enough of my staff reads *Gossip TO* that the cat is out of the bag."

"Did you tell them the truth?"

"Why would I do that?"

"Because no one in their right mind would ever believe that someone like you would get engaged to someone like me?" she said, pointing out the obvious.

"What is that supposed to mean?" He looked genuinely annoyed.

"Calm down. I didn't mean to insult you."

"You just meant to insult yourself?"

She held up her hands in a gesture of surrender. "I didn't mean anything other than that we're an unlikely couple." She could tell he was going to argue some more, so she stood up. "I have to get back to work. We can't all be CEOs who reschedule meetings at will."

He stood, too. "I told Lauren. No one else, though. It's none of their business."

"I thought she was looking at me strangely," Rosie said, moving toward the door.

He followed and held it for her. "I'll see you when you get home tonight."

"Oh, just spend a couple hours with Fifi, make sure she doesn't go crazy. She'll drop off around nine anyway. You don't have to stay until I get home."

He lifted those gorgeous gray-blue eyes and stared at her for a moment before he said, "I'm staying."

Chapter Six

"Oh, can it," said Marcus to Fifi as the canine howled her displeasure over being led back inside after their walk. Marcus couldn't even begin to think when he had last gone for a walk with no destination. Or the last time he'd left the office before nine o'clock, for that matter. Carla had about had a heart attack when he told her not to order dinner in for him as she usually did before she left.

Fifi howled again.

"Shut up."

She switched to barking.

"Yeah, well, try this on for size: dinner."

The barking turned happy then as Fifi wiggled her over-sized doggie butt excitedly.

Marcus refrained from pointing out that since she presumably had dinner every night after her walk, she shouldn't be so surprised. But only because that would mean he was trying to out-logic a beagle. A man had to have some standards, even if there was no one of the human variety around to observe him living up to them.

After he got Fifi settled and set up his laptop on Rose's dining room table, he took a little stroll around the apartment, scanning bookshelves (lots of science nonfiction and a bunch of novels he'd never heard of) and checking out the contents of the refrigerator (some Tupperwares that were probably full of the curry, tons of veggies in various states of decay, and about a hundred cans of Diet Coke).

He took in teal dining room chairs and an enormous crystal chandelier that had the odd pink crystal interspersed with the regular ones. Rose's space managed to have bold design flourishes at the same time that it radiated a homey, lived-in feeling. He was going to get into the website, but since he was on his snooping campaign, he wanted to have a look in her bedroom first. Which was wrong, he recognized. There was nothing in there that concerned him. But on the other hand, she'd never said *not* to go in her bedroom.

The bed, which was covered in a giant fluffy purple-and-white-striped duvet, was made, but haphazardly so. The wall above the bed was painted with stenciled letters, the kind you see in design magazines or in houses for sale that say things like "Dream" or "Love" or some shit like that. But this just said, "Action."

He burst out laughing. She had "Action" written above her bed?

What a weirdo.

He thought of her twirling in his arms at the Fall Ball, and he had to adjust his pants a bit.

What a compelling, gorgeous weirdo.

God, listen to him. He needed to get her out of his system.

When Rosie unlocked her apartment and pushed the door open, she initially thought Marcus had changed his mind and not waited for her. The apartment was dark and utterly silent. Which was a little disappointing.

Which was, in turn, a little alarming.

But then, just as her eyes were adjusting to the faint light coming from the dining room, he said, "Hey."

It was just a *hey*. One little syllable. But just like when he'd snuck up behind her at his office, it was a very…compelling syllable. Low and gravelly, he drew it out in a way that went straight to her core.

"How was the underage management consultant?"

She moved deeper into the apartment and set her keys on the table. He had moved a lamp from the living room and was ensconced in a circle of warm light. He wore his work clothes from earlier in the day but had lost the jacket and tie. He shot her a boyish grin, which was funny because he obviously wasn't a boy. There was the premature gray hair to start with. He was also decidedly not a boy at work. She had only observed him in his natural habitat for a short time, but it had been enough to see that he utterly commanded the situation.

Still, there was a vulnerability about him that she caught a flash of sometimes in the rebel who had broken from his father and forged his own path.

"How old are you?" she asked, not really caring that the question was abrupt and probably borderline rude.

He didn't seem flustered by it, though. "Forty."

She sat down. "The management consultant was fine."

"Just fine?"

"He was…" How to explain? "He was not forty."

"I told you he was a kid."

"Yeah, he kind of was. Not living in his parents' basement or anything—not that kind of kid. He was obviously very successful professionally. But he talked a lot about bands I'd never heard of. He was a bit of a music nerd. Not that that's a bad thing." She shrugged. There had been nothing overtly wrong with her date, and yet…

"But he didn't insult you like the last one. Or do anything creepy or unwelcome."

"No, not at all," she rushed to assure him because a fierceness had made its way into his tone. Apparently "fake fiancé" came with a dose of protectiveness. "He was very solicitous. He seemed into me, asked if he could kiss me, in fact."

"What? Just now? Outside?"

"No. We went to a restaurant in the beaches, and he suggested a walk on the boardwalk afterward. I think he was going for the big romantic gesture because he stopped us under this tree where you could see the moon over the lake."

Marcus shut his computer and began stacking some papers he had scattered around her table. "And?"

"It was kind of awkward, actually. The first kiss always is."

He stood and shoved his computer into a bag. "I myself am not a fan of the grand gesture brand of first kiss. That's not my M.O."

"Oh!" she exclaimed, following him toward the door. "You have moves!" For some reason, the idea of Marcus having a kissing philosophy, of him trying to impress a woman, surprised her. She would have thought he just had to exist for women to be interested in him. But... "I thought you didn't do relationships."

"I don't. But I'm not a monk. I keep things casual, though. I just make sure everyone knows the score. And as for my so-called *moves*, I just think people put too much stock in the big, all-important first kiss."

"You think so? Because—"

And then he was kissing her. Oh, God, Marcus was kissing her, his lips gentle, impossibly soft.

But then, as suddenly as he had started, he stopped. Which was oddly disappointing.

But he didn't pull away as his mouth left hers. "I'm more a fan of the low-key first kiss," he rasped, his lips brushing over her cheek as he spoke.

She was trying to calm her out of control heart, to think what to say, when he was back, framing her face with both his hands this time, pressing his lips a little more firmly against hers, letting his tongue test their seam. She was just about to open for him when—damn him!—he pulled back again.

"Disarm," he whispered, his lips moving against hers as he spoke. "You can talk while you're kissing, even." He trailed a few kisses along her jawline, saying, "Kissing doesn't have to be such a big deal," as he went. She was tempted to disagree, to point out that this was, in fact, a Very Big Deal, but she feared that to do so would make him stop. As each kiss deposited a tiny pinprick of electricity on its target, one part of her brain was aware that kissing the fake fiancé who didn't do relationships was a bad idea. But the other, bigger part couldn't remember why.

"There doesn't need to be a big, grand lead up for a kiss to be good," he went on, having made his way back to her lips and begun nipping the bottom one.

She kissed him this time, and just as her lips hit his, he murmured, "Exactly." And as she twined her hands around his neck, he pulled her closer, and she felt the unmistakable evidence of his arousal. He didn't try to hide it, like many men would during a first kiss. He also didn't try to rub it against her like other, creepier men would. It was just a fact between them—a very impressive fact—and the idea that it was her who'd inspired this response was intoxicating. *He* was intoxicating. *Disarm*, he'd said, but *dis-knee* was more like it because she had to concentrate harder than she would have liked for hers not to buckle under the assault of his mouth. His tongue was making incursions into her mouth, and one hand stroked down the side of her throat and grabbed hold of the neck of her shirt, as if he were trying to anchor her to him. It was maybe the sexiest thing that had ever happened to her, and she couldn't contain a moan of pleasure.

But she must have been mistaken to assume the shirt-grabbing gesture had been an anchoring one, because all of a sudden, he was gone.

The kiss was over.

She wanted to howl her protest. But there was no way to do that and retain any shred of dignity.

And damn him if he didn't then wink at her and say, "You have a letter to write, don't you? I'll talk to you later," before slipping out the door.

Chapter Seven

"What are you doing?"

"Shit." Marcus jumped, nearly spilling his coffee.

What Marcus had been doing when Lauren snuck up on him Friday evening in his office was staring at sketches for the new EcoHabitat home page. He had a lot more work to do on the sub-pages—he'd put together a map last night at Rose's place—but he wanted to get his broad vision for the main page down on paper.

Well, that wasn't strictly true. To an outsider, it would appear that Marcus was looking at sketches. What he was actually doing was staring blankly at them while his mind revisited the scene of him kissing Rose last night. Or her kissing him—he wasn't sure which.

Which was part of the problem. He'd meant to demonstrate that kissing could be casual. Low-stakes. But the fact that he had lost control of his little demonstration so much that he wasn't sure who had been in the driver's seat suggested that he had *not* proven his hypothesis.

And when she'd thrown her arms around his neck and pressed herself against his already rock-hard cock, he was pretty sure that responding by grabbing her shirt as if he were a caveman wasn't properly interpreted as a show of indifference. So when she added a low, breathy moan to the mix, he'd been forced to admit failure and call the whole thing off.

"You said to come by before I left if I had time."

Right. Lauren. He glanced at his watch. Eight o'clock. He tried to remember that not everyone worshipped at the altar of work as fervently as he did. "It's Friday. We can talk about this next week."

"It's all right," she said, sitting next to him at the table he'd been working at. "I am a loser who has no Friday night plans other than a date with my TiVo." He watched her take in the project he was working on. "Unless you and your *fiancée* do."

He sighed. "I told you, it's not real." He'd sworn her to secrecy, but he hadn't been able to resist telling *someone* the truth.

"Yeah, yeah. You're fake engaged to an Amazonian Mindy Kaling. Cry me a freaking river."

Here we go.

"Why didn't you tell me that she was stunning?"

"Because I was afraid you'd steal her away from me?" Marcus teased. "Oh, wait. I forgot. She's not gay."

"She's also not yours to begin with, so I'm not sure *steal* is the right word."

Touché.

"So, what?" Lauren went on. "You're redoing her website

to say thanks for helping me stick it to my old man?"

She wasn't wrong per se, but Marcus preferred to look at it from another, more comfortable, angle. "My mother was a huge supporter of EcoHabitat. I hadn't realized what a mess their website was. It's the least I can do."

"Well, give it to me, and I'll get one of the digital strategists going on it. We'll bring you some concepts next week."

"I'm doing it myself. Well, I'm doing architecture and art. I'm going to get Dax Harris to do the programming and bring in some of the copywriters for content."

There was a pause while Lauren reared back a little in her seat. Then she said, "Excuse me, what?"

He hadn't worked on the nuts and bolts of a project like this for years, and she knew it. And he could see her trying to make sense of the fact that he was planning to have the CEO of one of the neighboring companies, Cherry Beach Software Solutions, do the coding. So Marcus braced himself for the Inquisition. But she just said, "Okaaaay."

"I was hoping to bounce some ideas off you."

"Okay. We should catch up on Magnifique, too. Should I order a pizza?" She pulled out her phone and winked.

She was referencing the company's fledgling months, when it was just them, and they would work late into the night, subsisting on pizza and Chinese takeout. These days when they ordered in, it was usually from the high-end deli down the street.

Marcus felt a flash of gratitude. Neither he nor his art director was sentimental, and they didn't really hang out—long hours at the office meant they were already in each other's company a ridiculous number of hours per week—but she could be utterly trusted. He was lucky to have her.

And Dax, too. Marcus had only recently begun spending time with Dax and with Jack Winter. He'd always been friendly with the men who helmed the other two companies on the 49th floor, but it hadn't been until his mother died that he started to occasionally join them for a drink after work. It sounded corny, but losing his mother made him appreciate how fleeting everything was. Not that he was suddenly going to be swearing blood oaths to Lauren and the guys, but he'd decided it wouldn't kill him to have a little fun every now and then. Dax and Jack had been trying to get him to join their pickup hockey league, and he'd been resisting. But he wasn't sure why. He resolved to take them up on the offer. He hadn't skated since he was a kid, but he used to love it—until his father made him quit, citing a need to focus on his studies.

"Have you done a brief?" asked Lauren. "What are EcoHabitat's goals?"

"Yes," he said, sliding his iPad over to her. He had dutifully done all the planning required for a project like this—asking himself and answering questions related to goals, audience, and so on. But in truth, once he'd done it, he had set it aside. What had really been guiding him as he made his sketches was the image of Rose, sitting primly in her quaint little office in the attic at EcoHabitat. Or Rose, struggling to subdue a barking Fifi. He grinned. "Basically, we're trying to save the entire animal kingdom. And maybe some trees, too."

On Thursday afternoon, Rosie was just closing down her computer when Marcus appeared in the doorway of her office. "Hi!" she exclaimed, but then, fearing that the level of enthusiasm behind that "hi" was more appropriate for a real fiancé than a fake one—even one who could kiss like Marcus—she cleared her throat and tried again with a more casual, "What are you doing here?"

Rosie tried not to stare too openly at Marcus's mouth. It seemed unbelievable that he could be standing there, casually talking to her with that mouth, like he hadn't just been pressing it all over her a week ago. They hadn't talked since the kiss—hadn't even texted. Rosie had concluded that he really meant it when he said kisses didn't have to be a big deal. It was just that, personally, her interpretation tended more toward "big deal." And since she wasn't sure what the fake-fiancé-you-just-made-out-with protocol was, she'd returned his radio silence in kind. But now that he was here, acting like nothing had happened and no time had passed, she was a little annoyed.

"I thought I'd show you how the new site is coming," he said, answering the question she'd forgotten she asked.

"That's a lie." She hadn't heard from him all week, and he just happened to show up on Thursday afternoon? Just like last time she saw him—when he kissed her—had been a Thursday.

"Excuse me?" he drawled, channeling all the snobbery she had seen members of his family display.

She stood up and began packing her bag for home. "For some mysterious reason, you don't want me going on my Thursday night dates." She paused and regarded him. "Actually, I don't think it's so mysterious. You have some kind of perverse, bullshit macho thing going on where even though what's between us is fake, you still don't want me to be with anyone else."

"You're overthinking this, Rose. I just finished the architecture today, and I thought you might want to weigh in on it before I go any further."

"Oh." Geez, maybe she had been seeing motive where there was none—because why would someone like Marcus care what she did? How embarrassing. Heat flooded her cheeks as she shooed him into the hallway. "Well, I can't tonight. I have a date."

"Right," he said, leaning against the wall as she flipped off the hall lights. "We'll do it another time. You have Fifi covered for tonight?"

"Oh, I don't have Fifi anymore," Rosie said, ignoring the odd twist of disappointment in her gut. Where had that come from? Did she *want* Marcus sitting in her apartment like some paternalistic millionaire web-designing fairy godfather while she went on a date? "A spot opened up for her in the shelter."

"Okay, I'll just head back to the office then and talk—"

"I do have a new dog, though." *Just not one that requires babysitting*, she reminded herself sternly.

"Yeah? I tell you what. How about I come over and hang with the new dog. I'll do some more work on the site, and we can look at it after your date."

The idea was strangely compelling. A late night in her apartment with Marcus, going over site plans. It almost sounded like a date. Except not, she reminded herself. Because she actually *had* a date. "If you want to come over and babysit Rambo, I'm sure he'd love it. I would say I owe you, but…" She trailed off and waved her hand in the space between them, trying to make a joke to demonstrate how non-bothered she was by his commanding presence. "I guess we're even."

"Oh, just wait until you see what I have in mind for your site. You *will* owe me then."

He waited while she locked her door, and as they set off down the stairs, he mimicked her earlier motion of indicating the space between them. "Speaking of, I'm going to get you a ring for the Hanukkah dinner. What kind do you want?"

"Don't get me a ring!" Pretending to be engaged was one thing, pretending to be engaged with a *ring* quite another.

"No one in their right minds would believe I proposed to you and there's no ring. They're already talking about the lack of one at the ball. I told them we were having it sized."

She sighed. He was right. "Okay, well, it should be something fake." She threw a glance over her shoulder at him as he followed her out of the stairwell and through the cubicles that occupied the back of the first floor. "Like us."

Everyone stopped talking as they entered the space. Heads turned, just as they had when they'd walked through the cubicles at his office. But here, unlike at the Lakefront Centre, it wasn't because the employees were afraid of him. No, no, they were too busy gaping at him. She bit her lip so as not to laugh. Marcus, with his impeccable, tasteful suit and his conservative tie—today's was muted maroon with tiny gray stripes—was as out of place here as she had been on his turf. At EcoHabitat, the staff dressed business casual at best. And though the first floor of the old house was renovated, it still screamed "We got all this stuff at Ikea!" There were no hardwood floors or framed pieces of original art on the walls like at his office.

At least no one here besides Hailey had heard about the "engagement," so their staring wasn't directed at her. "Bye!" she called to her colleagues, waving over her shoulder as she led Marcus out the back door. "Oh, wait, is Nate here?" she asked, looking around for the dark car.

"Nope. I gave him the night off." His face was unreadable as he hailed a cab. She resisted pointing out that normal people got around the city by subway. But apparently when one's personal chauffeur had the night off, a taxi was already slumming it.

He opened the door for her and held out his hand like he was helping her into a carriage in a Jane Austen movie. That was Marcus for you. After giving the driver instructions, he turned to her. "Who's tonight's lucky guy?"

She perked up. "Dave. Thirty-three. Supply chain manager." He started to say something, but she held up her hand. "I know what you're going to say. It's another one of those jobs where normal people have no idea what it means. But I didn't even have to ask. In the same email where he said that's what he did, he explained it."

"And what did he say?"

"He asked if I'd ever gone to a store, and they didn't have my size. When I said yes, story of my life, he said it was his job to make sure that doesn't happen. Apparently he works for Walmart."

He started to wrinkle his nose, which got her back up. "Hey! We can't all be old-money millionaires." The moment it was out, though, she regretted her choice of wording. Marcus might be a millionaire—she was assuming based on the expensive suits and the private chauffeur—but he hadn't relied on his family's money for his success. To cover her discomfiture, she pulled out her phone and called up a photo of Dave.

Marcus raised his eyebrows. "Is he Indian? This should make your mother happy."

"He's half Indian, which might be good enough for Mom. I almost vetoed him because of it, in fact. But then I thought, that's kind of like reverse prejudice. I was rebelling for the sake of rebelling." She shot him a look. "Like someone else I know. So, viola! I'm meeting Dave at Red Lobster at seven."

"Dave from Walmart at Red Lobster. Sounds delightful."

She shot him a look. He could be so snooty sometimes. Apparently you could take the boy out of old money, but you couldn't take old money out of the boy. The car had pulled up to her building, and he waved away her attempt to pay the driver.

"I'm sorry," he said, after they'd begun the elevator ride up in silence.

She whipped her head around. What was he talking about? If he apologized for kissing her last week, she was going to break up with him. Or fake break up with him, or whatever. It wasn't worth the drama. She'd been hoping they could just pretend it never happened.

"I was being a snob just then. You should be free to go out where you want—and with whomever you want—without me interfering. And, anyway, Red Lobster is…great."

She blinked for a moment, unable to cover her surprise. Then, not knowing what to say, she punched him in the arm as a way of dispensing absolution. "Well, those cheddar biscuits *are* insanely good. But you have to stay away from those. They just fill you up, and…you have no idea what I'm talking about, do you?"

He shrugged.

He couldn't even pretend to be a man of the people. She shook her head and unlocked the door. Silence. Her newest foster pup was weird that way.

"Rambo?" she called, flipping on the light in the hallway. "Rambo, honey, I'm home." Soon enough, the tiny Yorkie peeked around the corner from the kitchen. "This dog is unnaturally silent," she whispered to Marcus. "He's a miniature terrier. He should be yapping up a storm."

Marcus looked amused as he shed his suit jacket and loosened his tie. "Rambo?"

She shrugged. "I like incongruous names. I think they're funny."

"What's his story?"

"A family came by to try to drop him off. They had a baby who'd developed allergies, they said. The shelter said they were full, but then they found Rambo in a crate on their steps the next morning."

"Wow."

"Yeah, and usually a silent dog is one who's been abused."

He furrowed his brow. "Well, those people need to learn to pick on someone their own size. This mutt isn't much bigger than a squirrel."

"It will turn out," she assured him. "Rambo will get snapped right up. He's adorable and silent. How often do you get that combination?"

She didn't miss the look he was giving her, like he was trying to hold in laughter.

"In a *dog*," she said, handing him a leash. "Will you take him down for a pee? He doesn't really need a walk—he's too much of a shrimp."

"Yeah, but we'll wait for you," Marcus said, moving over to the dining room table and taking his computer out of his bag. "We'll walk down with you."

It felt a little strange dolling herself up when she could hear Marcus puttering around just on the other side of the door. But she didn't want to be late, so she raced through pinning up her hair and threw on a swishy red dress, hoping Marcus would like it.

Hoping *Dave* would like it. *Dave.*

"Dave," she whispered the name out loud once more for good measure, slipping into a pair of electric blue heels.

When she stepped back into the living room, he was at the dining room table setting up the same lamp he'd pilfered last week. "I hope you don't mind that I've been moving this lamp. I hate overhead light when I'm—"

He stopped talking abruptly as he looked up. Then his gaze slid down her body, slowly. It would have been gross if she'd been subjected to it on the street, or in pretty much any other context. But now, she couldn't stop looking at his Adam's apple, which bobbed as he swallowed. Her skin started to prickle, and she had to order herself not to squirm under his appraisal.

His eyes paused at her feet for a moment, and she would have sworn they felt hot. So now she had to order herself not to squirm her *toes* inside her shoes.

"Damn," he said as his eyes began their journey upward, not even trying to hide the fact that he was checking her out. There was absolutely no subtlety about what he was doing, in fact. Probably this was part of his whole, "I'm a rich CEO dude, and the world bends to my will" thing.

The worst part was, she liked it.

Which was a thought to be examined later because she was on her way out to meet Dave. *Dave.*

Marcus let loose a low wolfish whistle. "Dave is going to choke on his delicious cheddar biscuit."

She wasn't sure what to say to that. What did one say when one's fake fiancé proclaimed one so hot that one's actual date was going to meet an untimely end?

She was saved from having to come up with something when he said, "Why do your shoes never match your outfit?"

"Oh!" She looked down at the blue shoes, startled. "I don't know! The non-matchy-matchy look is sort of popular now, but I've been doing it forever. It's kind of my signature thing, although I never thought of it that way until Hailey *told* me it was my signature thing. And then, of course, once you have a signature thing, you're sort of stuck with it." She shrugged, realizing that that long, rambling explanation probably just made her seem flighty. "I don't know. It's probably stupid. I should just grow up and dress like a normal person."

"No."

She'd been looking at her shoes again, but his objection was so sharp that she whipped her eyes back to his face. His eyes were burning with...something.

"It suits you," he rasped, bending over and clipping on Rambo's leash.

Dave.

Right. Dave time.

Marcus was startled to hear a key in Rose's lock a mere forty-five minutes later. He'd only just gotten back, fed Rambo, and settled down with his work. He half expected it to be someone else—a cleaner, a neighbor, someone she'd forgotten was stopping by.

But no, even in the dim light of the entryway, he could see the rainbow that was Rose in her red dress and blue shoes.

"Everything okay?" he asked, getting up to take the bags she was juggling as she shrugged out of her coat.

"Yeah, yeah." She kicked off her shoes in the entryway, and Marcus had to admit he was sorry to see them go. "I had to invoke the deal-breaker clause right off the bat. Not that I said it like that." She took one of the bags back from him. "I got Thai food, though, if you want some."

He tried to imagine what offense Dave could have committed that would cause her to flee immediately. Could there be anyone worse than TallDoctor? His fists flexed. "What did he do?"

She paused in the midst of uncorking a bottle of red wine. "He pulled up in a Hummer. I'm sorry, but I just cannot tolerate that."

He laughed. That was about the last thing he expected her to say. "Hummers don't have sterling environmental records, do they?"

"You can say that again. But in this case, it was also personal. I once got hit on my bike by a Hummer. I was okay, but the asshole hit and ran." She cocked her head. "Could have been Dave for all I know."

"You're a cyclist?" He was having trouble picturing it.

"Don't look so surprised." She pulled down a plate from

a cupboard. "You want some of this?" Then she pulled down a wineglass. "And/or some of this?"

"I'm not surprised." Okay, he was surprised. "I'm just…"

"I ride to work. Just not in the winter."

How…unexpected. But he should know by now that unexpected was the name of the game with Rose. "Do you ride in your normal work clothes, or do you change once you get there?"

She shot him a bewildered look as she started opening the various containers she'd spread out on the table. Okay, so probably that question was a little too…specific than was called for. It's just that the image of her riding along, skirt flapping in the wind, her heels hooked over the pedals—it did something to him.

"I pretty much just ride in my work clothes." He'd never answered her question about whether he wanted to eat with her, but she handed him a plate anyway. "It's not an Olympic sport, Marcus. It's just a mode of transportation."

"I know. It's just that I'm a bit of an enthusiast myself."

"Really?" That perked her up.

"I used to be anyway. I don't ride to work, obviously," he said, as she knew about Nate. "But I do enjoy a weekend ride." Or he had, even in the early days of the agency. But in truth, he couldn't remember the last time he'd gone for a ride.

She was making little piles of rice on her plate and carefully plopping servings of various dishes over each pile. "I'm telling you," she said as she broke open a pair of wooden chopsticks, "when he pulled up in that beast, he might as well have been wearing a shirt that said, *I have a tiny penis.*"

"Really?" he said, choking on laughter as he loaded his

own plate.

"Nothing says masculine overcompensation like a Hummer. I'm sorry, Dave, but you ride up on one of those things, and I'm gonna fake an emergency so fast you won't even have time to park that beast."

Still chuckling, he followed her into the dining room. "But that's probably not a screening question on your dating website." Leave it to Rose. Most people's deal breakers were things like smoking or living with parents.

"It should be." She flopped into a chair. "Because obviously, the questions they do have aren't working."

"You do seem to be having a streak of bad luck. You must be doing it wrong."

"Doing it wrong?" she echoed through a mouthful of mango salad. "How can you do it wrong? All you do is answer a bunch of questions and stick a photo up. It's not like I'm going to *lie* on Match.com, given that I'm actually looking for, you know, a *match*."

He slid his iPad over. "Pull up your profile. Let's have a look."

She paused in her chewing, wary, but took the iPad, messed with it for a minute, then slid it back to him.

It was strange to see her profile. He knew she was looking for a guy, but to see it advertised so blatantly was a little disquieting. He forced himself to focus, though God knew why he was trying to help her with this. Hadn't he just been trying to *stop* her from going out on her internet dates? It was just he hated to see her with these loser guys she was coming up with. She deserved better. "Okay, so right off the bat, I can see a problem. You say you're looking for someone twenty-five to thirty-three. That's a pretty narrow range."

"You were the one mocking the immaturity of the management consultant. I'm not going below twenty-five."

"That's not what I mean. You should make the upper limit older."

"I figured if I was going four years younger than I am, it was hypocritical and anti-feminist to go more than four years older on the other end of the scale." She wrinkled her nose. "Plus, if the guy gets too old, it just seems kind of... gross."

He narrowed his eyes and shot her a skeptical look. "I'm forty. Do I seem too old for you?" Then he added, "Hypothetically." Because that's how he meant it.

She shifted in her seat, suddenly restless. Good. "I guess not."

"Okay, so that's one thing to change. Now, you say you're not into sports."

"Because I'm *not*," she declared.

"But you're a cyclist."

"I *told* you," she said. "It's a mode of transportation. I don't really do it for fun. I am not even remotely what a reasonable person would call sporty."

She was getting annoyed with his meddling, but he didn't care. "Yes, but let's say you were settled down with a guy who, for example, played hockey once a week." He was thinking of Dax and Jack and their girlfriends, neither of whom were particularly sporty either. "How would you feel about that?"

She cocked her head, considering. "Fine, I guess." Then she laughed. "Especially if it got him away from the house for an evening. I'm looking for a boyfriend, not a ball and chain."

"Right, you could have a girls' night. Or solitude. Or you could even come to the occasional game. Make an evening of it—bring hot chocolate in a thermos, the whole deal."

"Can there be Bailey's in the hot chocolate?"

He grinned. "There can. My point is that it's good to look for someone who has hobbies, independent interests. There's nothing that dooms a relationship faster than being too dependent on the other person."

"I do not disagree. And how'd you get so wise, Mr. I-Don't-Do-Relationships?"

He ignored the question. "All right, so most guys are into sports. Crossing sports off your list is going to eliminate a lot of contenders."

"I see your point."

"So, moving on. You say in the free text that you're looking for a guy who's not married to his job."

"And I stand by that. There's more to life than work. We all have to supplicate ourselves at the altar of capitalism to a certain extent, but I don't like people who are totally defined by their jobs. You know?"

He did not know. He firmly believed that if you wanted something, you had to be all in. The Rosemann Agency would not exist had Marcus not been married to his job in those early years. Hell, he was still having a pretty serious affair with it. But he thought it unwise to argue. And he *was* joining Dax and Jack's hockey team, so it wasn't like he had *nothing* else going on. But maybe she had a point. He should recreate more, or…do whatever people who weren't workaholics did—how did they fill all those hours? Regardless, this was not about him. This was *most decidedly* not about him. "I think you're being too prescriptive. Every precariously employed loser who lives in his mother's basement is going to read that as an endorsement."

She twirled a chopstick between her thumb and forefinger. "I've had an okay run lately on the employment front, but I will admit that I had a spate of guys this past summer who were either trying to write a novel or had been in grad school for an alarming number of years."

"I rest my case."

The chopstick had made its way to her mouth, where she chewed on it as she squinted at him, like he was a puzzle.

"What?"

She drew the now-damp chopstick from her mouth, slowly. Painfully slowly. "I just realized that with my current profile, you would never make the cut. You're too old, you're obsessed with your job, and apparently you're a cyclist. But with all these fixes, you'd be in."

Was she suggesting that he'd somehow engineered this? That he'd advised against the very changes that had been excluding him? Because that was ridiculous. He was merely applying common sense. "Finally," he said, choosing not to answer and enlarging her profile photo instead. "I think your biggest problem is that this picture is all wrong."

"What?" She actually recoiled, and he felt a twinge of dismay that he'd hurt her feelings. He was going soft.

"The picture itself is fine—you look good." She really did. It was a head and shoulders shot, and it looked like it had been taken in her office. "It's just that this picture does not send the message you want it to send. You look too professional. This is a shot you could have on your LinkedIn profile."

She winced. "I actually do have that on my LinkedIn profile."

"Exactly. Are you done eating?" When she nodded, he tugged her to her feet and led her to the sofa. "Let's take a new one."

"What? No! I get where you're coming from, and I'll post a new shot, but—"

"Sit," he commanded, pointing to the middle of the sofa. She had turned on the hall light when she came in, and he moved to turn it off. Then he went to retrieve the table lamp he'd moved to the dining room. When he returned it to its home on one of the sofa's end tables, she was still standing where he'd left her. "Sit," he said again.

She sat.

He assessed the scene. The warm, low light was good. He took a couple of the pillows that littered the couch and stuffed them behind her. "Now pull your knees up on the sofa and sit back against the pillows, like you're lounging casually."

She did as he asked, though her eyebrows were in permanent raised-skeptical mode.

He stepped back, assessing. "Okay, now turn your body a little so I'm not shooting you head on. That's nobody's best angle."

She obeyed without comment, which surprised him.

They were almost there. He set down the iPad. As he approached, she leaned out of his way.

"Don't move," he said, lowering himself onto the sofa next to her and sliding his fingers into her hair.

"What are you—oh! Oh my God, that feels amazing."

He'd been aiming to muss her hair. It was looking a little too tame, but he'd triggered an almost-feline response in her as she let her head roll back. He pressed his fingers more firmly against her scalp, and her mouth fell open as she moaned.

This was going to be a problem.

Rose was looking for The One. He was most decidedly not that—he wasn't anyone's The One. He was trying to *help* her find The One with this stupid profile, for God's sake. His usual M.O. with women was to make sure they knew the score, have some fun, and move on once it wasn't fun anymore. But something about Rose made him loath to do that, to wreck everything about their weird friendship when he walked away, as he would eventually have to do.

And yet...his dick wasn't responding to logic.

Her eyes were closed, as if the pleasure his fingers brought to her scalp was too much to witness, but suddenly she sat up straighter, shaking her head as if to dislodge his fingers. "Sorry about that. I lost my head for a moment there. Ha! No pun intended."

He wished he could shake his own head to expel the image of her from his mind's eye. Because right now, with her red dress, her messy hair, her warm brown skin almost golden in the soft light—not to mention that look she was giving him that was a cross between wicked and mischievous—he couldn't imagine any guy looking at her profile and not prostrating himself at her feet.

"Let's do this," she said, messing up her hair even more with one hand and using the other to bring her wineglass to her lips. She took a long, deep drink. He watched her throat work as she swallowed. "I get what you're going for here, and why the hell not?" She leaned back against the cushions and let her mouth fall open a little. "Do I look suitably sexed up?"

Yes. Yes she did.

But he didn't say that out loud, just swiped through the iPad to the camera app.

"It's probably better if you stand up, right? And I'll look up at you like you're the big manly man?" She picked up a pillow and peeked out from behind it playfully so that just her eyes—and that criminally long hair—were visible.

"Hold still," he said, suddenly peevish.

Ignoring him, she continued to vamp it up, tossing the pillow aside and leaning forward and squeezing her arms together to showcase her cleavage. "How's this?" Laughing, she let one of the straps of her dress fall down her shoulder, like she thought she was doing a parody of the idea of a sexpot. Except it wasn't a parody.

Good God, it was too much. He hadn't stood up before when she suggested it, but now he did. He didn't bother taking a step back from her either. He just let her come face to face—in a manner of speaking—with what she did to him.

The laughing stopped immediately.

Good. He futzed with the settings on the shot, then held up the tablet.

She was looking at the camera as if she could see *through* it, to him. If he didn't know better, he'd say she looked like she'd spent the day in bed. And yet, there wasn't the sense of satiation that one would expect to see if that had been the case.

No, quite the reverse, actually. She looked like she wanted to devour him.

And if that look translated in the photo he was about to take, he'd have to set her up with her own personal security detail as soon as she posted it to her account.

Slowly, slowly, he lowered the iPad so that there was

nothing between them.

She raised her eyebrows questioningly.

"Change of plans," he said, the sound of his own voice unfamiliar, raspy and lower than usual.

"Oh?" she said, and there was a challenge in that single syllable.

He dropped the iPad on the coffee table. He sure as hell wasn't taking a picture of her like that to post on the internet for a bunch of basement-dwelling Neanderthals to jerk off to.

There was a standoff then. A silent one. But they didn't need words to know what was going to happen next. The only question was who was going to cave first.

Him. It was going to be him.

It was the last coherent thought he had before he lunged.

She was ready for him because she caught him—not just with her arms, but with those long legs, which she proceeded to wrap around him as they fell back onto the sofa.

"This is probably a bad idea," she whispered before she kissed him.

He could only grunt because she opened her mouth, and if she thought he wasn't going to seize that opportunity, she was crazy. He would have preferred to exercise more control, but with his hands tangled in her hair and the smell of her flooding his senses, it was impossible. So he surrendered, and plunged his tongue into her mouth, which was—*God*—so soft and hot. And there were those legs, wrapped around his waist as if she was afraid he would flee otherwise. It made him crazy, the idea of her wanting him as much as he wanted her.

When he dragged his lips from hers, she gave a little wail of protest that went straight to his cock, making it even harder, which he would not have thought possible a moment ago.

He moved to remedy the situation by sliding his lips down her throat and across her collarbone. He was rewarded with a low moan as she stretched her neck out like a cat, as if to give him better access.

When he added a hand, kneading her breast through the fabric of her dress, she jerked and gasped, as if she were suffocating, which he knew she was not because her chest was heaving.

"Yes," he agreed, finally answering her earlier question. "This is a really bad idea. We should probably stop." He wasn't sure why, but he wanted to tease her. Bait her a little. Possibly because this whole encounter was making him feel so reckless. So out of control, and he wanted to seize some back.

When he accompanied his declaration with a cessation of all movement, she snapped her head up. "Like hell," she whispered, lifting her torso off the sofa a bit in order to move her breast under his stilled hand.

When he still didn't move, she sat up and lightly bit his lower lip.

Which, he had to admit, startled the hell out of him. But also made him fear he would come in his pants.

"We're engaged, remember?" she whispered, kissing the spot she'd just bitten. The contrasting sensations in such quick succession were nearly enough to send him over the edge.

"You make a very good point," he said, reaching around and peeling her legs off him so he could pull her upright. If this was going to continue, he had to slow things down. Touch her without letting her touch him.

Once he had her upright—and pouting, for she must have thought him tipping them into a vertical position meant their little interlude was over—he knelt on the floor between her legs. "Patience," he whispered as he lowered his mouth to her throat, raking his stubbly cheek against the already reddened skin there.

Since she had already let one of the straps of her dress fall, all he had to do was reach in and gather a handful of flesh and move it up while he pushed down the strapless bra she was wearing. He paused for a moment to admire her. Hell, *admire* wasn't a strong enough word. Before, when he'd been standing and she sitting and looking up at him with her sex kitten act, he'd thought she was the hottest thing he'd ever seen. It turned out the angle didn't matter at all. From this vantage point, she was a head taller than him, and, more importantly, she had abandoned all acting. Her eyes were glazed with what he flattered himself was desire, and her dress was hiked up around her waist and ruched down where he'd pulled it from her chest. One perfect brown-tipped breast taunted him, standing at attention and practically begging for his mouth.

He thought, for the second time, that she looked like a goddess. But instead of a hapless mortal worshiping at her feet, he was a consort being granted a temporary god status.

And he'd be damned if he was going to waste an opportunity like that. So he went straight for that dark, hard nub, closing his mouth around it as he kneaded the flesh beneath it upward.

"Oh my God," she breathed, writhing beneath his mouth.

He let his other hand rest on her leg. She was wearing tights, and when he rubbed his hand back and forth against her thigh, a satisfying friction resulted. But not as satisfying as the feeling of her bare skin against his hand would be.

Did he dare?

She must have been reading his mind because she lifted her hips up off the sofa, a clear invitation. So he let go of her breast, relishing the cry of disappointment that resulted, reached up to grab the waistband of her tights, and pulled. He'd been planning to pull them all the way off, but it was impossible not to be distracted by the sight of two bare, light brown thighs falling open, a pair of emerald green panties between them.

He hadn't paid any attention to her bra earlier, other than to shove it out of his way, but those green panties, in addition to just about killing him, planted in him an irresistible impulse to see if the bra matched. He wasn't normally the kind of guy who gave a shit about lingerie. If you were doing things right, he'd always believed, it all ended up on the floor anyway. But the idea that she was wearing bright green underwear under her red dress…and those blue shoes.

He had to know, so he lifted his gaze. She was sitting there with her tights around her knees and the front of her dress gaping open, so screw it, he was just going to find out. So he kneeled up, which put them roughly eye to eye. He didn't ask, just reached out and slid the other strap of her dress down her shoulder and pulled the fabric down enough to expose…a bright green bra that matched the panties.

A rogue thought slipped into his mind. "Was this for Dave?"

"What do you mean?" Confusion joined the desire that had been present in her face.

"Did you wear this little number"—he let his finger slide inside the bra and then pulled the edge of the fabric away from her skin before letting it fall back—"hoping that Dave would get to enjoy it?" They had talked a lot about her bad dates. He was suddenly realizing that they never talked about what happened on the not-bad ones. She had referenced one guy lasting three weeks, hadn't she? What had happened during those three weeks?

"And what if I did?"

The question, along with the fact that confusion was giving way to irritation on her face, snapped him back to reality. What the hell was the matter with him that he was letting a small piece of fabric unhinge him? Even if it had been for Dave, where was Dave now? Riding off into the sunset in his Hummer *without* the girl. "I suppose that would be none of my business," he answered. Because Rose was looking for a relationship, and he was not that guy.

"That's one thing we agree on, then," she said, straightening her spine and righting her dress, covering the green bra and the gorgeous breast — the breast that had been inside his mouth a moment ago. It seemed criminal. But he could not credibly object.

"I'm sorry," he said. "I got carried away." He didn't know if he was talking about his reaction to the bra just now — or the whole interlude. Maybe both.

She looked at him for a long moment. He thought maybe she was going to say, "It's okay, I got carried away, too." But instead she just looked at him evenly, her face no longer readable, and said, "It's late."

It was, of course, no such thing, her date having ended before it even began, but he nodded. He knew when he was being dismissed. He had work to do anyway. He'd spent enough time shirking his responsibilities because of Rose.

She stood up and stepped around him and his still-rock-hard dick. "It's late, and I have a letter to write."

Chapter Eight

The next morning, in the middle of her seventeenth draft of a text to Marcus telling him to call off the fake engagement, Rosie received an incoming one from him.

Come on a bike ride with me tomorrow.

That was it. She waited for more. But what was she waiting for? Another apology? After he'd left last night—and after she'd calmed down—she came to the conclusion that he probably hadn't meant any harm. They'd both gotten carried away. But the comment about Dave had stung. What stung even more was that she cared what Marcus Rosemann of "Marcus's Girls," Mr. I-Don't-Do-Relationships thought of her. As if she owed him any accounting of her sexual habits. Or her underwear-wearing habits. Or whatever. But even if he did apologize again, where would that leave them? Even if his intentions weren't bad, she was tired of being the convenient companion or…whatever she was, when in reality she was about as far from his type as it was possible to be. A non-Jewish, commitment-minded, vegetarian, slutty, color-blind peasant, in other words.

So why hadn't she sent any of those seventeen texts calling it all off?

Why was her finger hovering even now, waiting for him to say more?

Her body knew the answer, even if her brain was trying to take the high road.

I'll bring the sketches for the EcoHabitat site I meant to show you last night.

When, paralyzed with indecision, she still didn't reply, another text arrived.

Come on. You can break up with me. I'll bring the ring for you to throw back in my face. But I need your approval before I can continue with the site.

She sighed and started typing.

You'll still do the site if I break up with you?

The reply came right away.

Yes.

Rosie groaned audibly.

I don't have a mountain bike. I have a very girly city bike.

She knew he would interpret that text correctly—as capitulation.

Of course you do. Don't worry, we'll do the Leslie Spit. Very flat, paved.

"What is your damage?" Hailey plopped down on the guest chair in Rosie's office. "You're sighing like someone just died."

"I think my dignity is about to, so that's not too far off the mark," said Rosie as she read Marcus's instructions on where and when to meet.

"You're going to have to be more specific when it comes to potential dignity-threatening scenarios." Hailey smirked. "Is this about last night? Because I'm here for the debrief. How was Dave the supply chain manager?"

Rosie felt her cheeks heat. It was about last night, but of course, not in the way Hailey thought. "Um, no. Last night was another fail." In more ways than one. "I was actually talking about the fact that I just agreed to go biking with Marcus tomorrow."

"Oh, God, is his family athletic? Yuck. Family bike ride! Tell me the scary dad won't be there. I have to tell you, I pictured the Rosemanns more as golfers. Or, like, lacrosse players."

"No, no," said Rosie weakly, bracing herself for the attack she knew was coming. "It's just going to be Marcus and me."

Hailey blinked rapidly. "So you're going on a date."

"No! It's not a date."

"But you're hanging out independently of the whole fool-the-family charade."

There was no way to deny it. "Yes."

"So it's a date."

"It is not," she protested.

"It is, too."

"Hailey! Get out of here! I have stuff to do!" *Namely, send the world's most epic email to Jo.*

"Enjoy your *date!*" Hailey waggled her eyebrows as she stood to leave, but then she popped her purple fauxhawked head back inside the office, her face having grown serious. "Don't fall in love with him, though, Rosie. He's outright told you he's not a relationship guy. That's just a recipe for heartbreak."

Rosie rolled her eyes at her friend, but she knew.

She knew.

R osie was nervous as hell when she pedaled up to the foot of the Leslie Street Spit the next day.

She was also still dogged by the question that had consumed her all morning: what does one wear to a non-date outing in December with one's fake fiancé during which one will ride a bike and also discuss a web design project that one is attempting to slide by one's incompetent boss? In the end, she'd just decided on jeans, flat ankle boots, and a winter coat. It was an unseasonably warm, snowless December, but it would still be cold down by the lake.

She half expected Marcus to show up wearing one of his signature suits.

But no. He was not wearing a suit. It should have been impossible, but Saturday Marcus looked even better than Corporate Marcus. As evidenced by the fact that as she rolled to a stop next to him, she wanted to jump off her bike and tackle him. He was dressed in jeans and a dark gray pea-coat, and there was that damned stubble again. And Rosie, she had a thing for stubble. Not beards, but a good few days' worth of scruff was her kryptonite. And Marcus's was so… compelling. If the hair on his head was pepper with a touch of salt, his beard was the reverse, silver with dark accents.

It should have made him look older. Instead, it brought to mind what he would look like on, say, a Sunday morning. Waking up in bed after forty-eight hours away from his razor. Perhaps the sun would be streaming into his bedroom, glinting off those silver whiskers, whiskers that would feel amazing on—

"I like your coat." He flicked her sleeve.

Busted in the middle of that ridiculous fantasy, her face heated despite the cold. "Yeah, I call this my crazy coat," she said, looking down at herself. The dark purple wool was respectable enough, but the ruffles, not to mention the huge white faux fur cuffs—and fur-trimmed hood that was so big it fit over her bike helmet—had, in her mind, given the coat its nickname.

"So your other coat is your sober coat?"

"Well, not really," she said. "My other coat is pink. But it doesn't have ruffles."

He smiled. She realized that things were not weird be-tween them like she would have expected. She didn't know whether to be comforted or irritated by the fact because for God's sake, the man had had his mouth on her boob not two days ago.

"You ready?" he asked.

"As ready as I'll ever be."

They set off along the long finger of land that extended

out into Lake Ontario. Rosie had always known it was there, but somehow, never visited. What could she say? She wasn't sporty, as they had already established.

They rode at a leisurely pace in silence for a few minutes. Rosie took what felt like the first deep breath she'd had in days. Because it had yet to snow this winter, the leaves crunched under their wheels, and the brisk lake air was invigorating. A flock of birds flew low, and she shrieked and laughed, ducking as she rode.

"This is supposedly a bird sanctuary," said Marcus, who was keeping pace beside her. "I would think this would be right up your alley."

"You want to know a secret?" she said, feeling a little guilty for what she was about to confess. "I don't actually like birds."

"Ah! Busted!"

"I mean, I don't have anything against them," she rushed to qualify. "And of course, intellectually, I get that migratory patterns are important and all that."

"So this project you're shaking me down for. What you're saying is that you don't give a shit about it."

She whipped her head around because he had been speaking in such a deadpan tone that she panicked for a moment that he was truly pissed—and, as a donor, wouldn't he have a right to be? But his eyes danced.

"Of course I do! It's just that, personally, birds don't give me the warm fuzzies the way..." She trailed off, her mind wanting to finish the sentence with, *the way you do*.

"The way actual warm, fuzzy creatures do," he said instead.

She laughed. "Pretty much."

They kept going in companionable silence for a while until they reached the end of the line.

"But I do know my birds, even if I'm not particularly a fan," Rosie said as they dismounted and walked to the edge of the water. "See those weird-looking trees?" She pointed to a wooded area on an island several hundred yards out in the lake.

"Yeah."

"Even in the summer, those trees are totally stripped of leaves. There's a species of bird called the double-crested cormorant that destroys them. They'd almost gone extinct, but they were brought back from the brink. But they also eat a pound of fish a day—each of them. So they're decimating fish stocks."

"And trees, apparently. What's with that?"

"They have this crazy toxic poop that kills trees and groundcover."

He laughed out loud. "Crazy toxic poop—sounds like the name of a band. But I guess it's a serious problem?" he asked, leading her to a bench. "Let's sit for a minute."

"Yeah, and arguably, they're pushing out other native birds. Well, at least some people say that."

"So it's not a simple black and white thing, where these birds that were going to go extinct are suddenly back, and it's a victory."

"Yes!" she exclaimed. Other than Dr. Jill and a couple others in the EcoHabitat office, few people seemed to grasp the nuances of their work. "And it's a great example of how ecosystems are not simple things that can be easily boiled down to straightforward cause and effect."

"But shades of gray are harder to sell," he said

thoughtfully.

"That's right. In truth, it's not as simple as give us your money and we'll save Mother Nature. You sometimes never know, when you try to rebuild ecosystems, what's going to happen." She gestured at the denuded trees.

"You should be running that place, not Tony Carroll."

Whoa. Where had that come from? She shook her head and waved the compliment away, but secretly, it thrilled her.

"Here's a crazy idea." He rummaged around in his pannier and produced a sketch pad and gestured her to a bench. Settling himself beside her, he opened it to show her a hand-drawn sketch of a tree with the EcoHabitat logo. "I was thinking we'd do something like this, but—"

"I had no idea you would do this by hand."

"Old habit. And I won't really do it by hand. I have some wireframes to show you on the laptop, but I usually like to sketch the initial idea—the top layer—by hand." He pulled out a pencil and flipped to a blank page. "But now I'm thinking, every environmental charity on the planet probably uses something green. What if the landing page was those stark, denuded trees instead?" Nodding toward the trees in front of him, he started sketching. "It's a bit counterintuitive, but I think it could work as a bold artistic choice with the right words over it."

"I love it!" she cried. He looked up, startled, but then grinned. She hadn't realized how loud she was being, but damn, she also hadn't realized how talented Marcus was. "Instead of showing people what they'd expect from an organization like ours—trees, animals—we show them the consequences of not acting."

"Exactly." He kept looking at her. "I'm meeting some

friends tonight at Edward's—a bar in the financial district. One of them is Dax Harris, the CEO of another company in the Lakeview Centre. He's going to do the programming for your site. You should come. We can look at the wireframes and talk a bit."

"You're getting a CEO to do my programming." Wow. Marcus did not mess around. "I'm sure I could find a programmer who's a little less...important."

"Nah, I want this to be right."

"I feel like EcoHabitat should pay him for his time at least. Or maybe he needs a fake fiancée?"

Marcus grinned. Man, he was all smiles today. It was weird. "Nope, he owes me—I hooked him up with some investors recently for an app he's developing. And anyway, he most decidedly does not need a fake fiancée. He's got a real girlfriend he can't keep his hands off of. It's kind of gross, actually."

"Darn. And here I was thinking maybe it would be fun to two-time you." It was so easy to tease Marcus out here, away from the real world.

"He's a pro. You'll like him. And hey—it will be good practice for Hanukkah."

The idea of hanging out with Marcus and his friends was strangely alluring. Would he be Mr. Smiles with them, too? She felt like she was just beginning to see another side to Marcus. To peel the layers of the onion back a little. But... "I have a date tonight. A promising one—he's a classics professor."

His face shuttered so absolutely, she almost wondered if she'd been imagining his sunny countenance earlier. "It's not Thursday."

"I know. But the guy seemed great, and he's going out of town, so—"

"Break it," he interrupted.

"I can't."

He shut his sketchbook. "Can't or won't?"

"Does it matter?" she asked, to remind herself as much as anything. As tempting as the prospect of playing tourist in Marcus's life was, she had to remember that a tourist was all she would ever be. An actor. Hired for her unsuitability. So, no, she couldn't and wouldn't break tonight's date on his account. "Speaking of," she said, standing and brushing off her jeans. "I should go."

"Hang on." He grabbed her arm and tugged her back down onto the bench. "I have something for you first." He took off his glove and dug around in the front pocket of his jeans. She looked down at his closed fist, which was obscuring whatever it was he'd retrieved.

"Rose," he said, eyes dancing with merriment, his irritation of a moment ago no longer in evidence. "Will you marry me?"

He was joking, of course, but she couldn't contain a gasp as he opened his hand to reveal a stunning ring. It was a pink gem of some sort set in white gold or platinum. It was simple, stark even. But large. Bold. As if it had nothing to hide, no desire to be flanked by lesser gems.

Exactly to her taste.

"This was my mother's," he said.

"Oh my God, you can't give me a family heirloom. I told you to get something fake," she said, even as a part of her lamented the loss of the beautiful ring. But that was dumb, because you couldn't lose something that wasn't yours to begin with.

"It's not an heirloom. My mother bought it for herself the day my father told her he wanted a divorce, which was only a year and a half ago."

That made sense, because although the ring had a timeless quality about it, it didn't look vintage. Still, she couldn't take it, and started to say so, but Marcus wasn't paying attention to her—he was looking at the ring.

"She wore it on her right hand. She said it was her symbol of a new era of independence." He turned to her, pinning her with those blue-gray eyes. "It reminded me of you."

"It really is lovely," she said, letting him slip it on her finger. "What kind of stone is it? Tourmaline?"

"It's a pink diamond. Two carats, I believe."

"Holy crap, Marcus!" She started shaking her hand like the ring was a spider. "If it's not an heirloom, it's a future heirloom. I can't wear this! I'll just wear it to Hanukkah—give it to me then."

"Nah, just take it now," Marcus said. "Honestly, what am I going to do with it? I was her only child, and it's not like I'm going to wear it. It's just sitting in a safe deposit box. You might as well enjoy it for a while."

Well, heck, who was she to argue? She held her hand out to admire it. Then she turned to Marcus. "Thank you." The ring, in addition to being gorgeous, had also managed to puncture the tension that had settled on them when Marcus had asked her to break her date. "I do have to leave, though."

Marcus nodded but held her back. "One more thing."

"Yes?"

He swiveled to look at the lake. "I really am sorry about Thursday night."

Sorry you made out with me or sorry it got weird?

"Because of course your, ah…social life is none of my business. It won't happen again."

What won't happen again? she wanted to ask. Him going all Incredible Hulk jealousy monster or…the other stuff? Because the prospect of the latter not happening was sharply, strangely disappointing.

He still wasn't looking at her. Oh, man, he was really uncomfortable, which was so uncharacteristic for him that it made *her* uncomfortable. She decided to put him out of his misery and waved her hand dismissively. "Don't worry about it. And, for the record, I wasn't wearing that underwear for Dave." Why she added that unnecessary qualifier, she couldn't say.

He transferred his attention from the lake back to her, his eyes blue lasers homing in on her. There was the Marcus she knew, all cocky self-confidence and barely contained power. He licked his lips and let his eyes fall pretty blatantly to her boobs, as if he was trying to see her underwear beneath all her layers of clothing. She shivered, and it wasn't from the cold.

"Well," he finally said, once his eyes had traveled down the full length of her body and back up, "Dave doesn't know what he's missing."

Chapter Nine

After Rosie got home from the bike ride, her mom called and announced she was coming over. That wasn't unusual in and of itself, but generally her mother made a federal case out of planning everything at least a week in advance. She meticulously prepared not only food for them to eat for dinner, but several meals to leave with Rosie, all packed into a rolling suitcase. It was funny; the lunches her mother packed when she was a kid helped mark her as an oddball in their suburb. But now, the mere sound of that suitcase bumping over the sidewalk made her salivate.

So the fact that the matriarch had simply called and said, "I'm coming for dinner—cook something," was pretty much unprecedented. Enough so that Rosie called her date and switched their planned dinner to later-in-the-evening drinks.

Rosie could tell the moment her mother stepped off the train that something was up. Not only did she not fuss over the price of a taxi—the suitcase was huge, so they always took a cab, but not before having the same argument about the extravagance of doing so—she hadn't brought any luggage at all beyond her purse.

"Mom? What's wrong?" said Rosie gently as the taxi pulled away from the station.

"We'll discuss it when we get to your apartment."

Rosie started to really worry then. Was everything okay with her brother, who was away at college? She knew it was useless to press, though. Her mother would talk when she was good and ready.

And apparently she was good and ready the moment the door to Rose's apartment shut behind them. "I had a phone call from someone named Rachel Lowe," she announced, standing there with her coat on, still as a statue. "She was Marcus Rosemann's aunt, she said. Like I was supposed to know who Marcus Rosemann was."

Shitballs! Triple shitballs!

"Mom, I can explain." But could she? *So there's this guy, see. I'm pretending to be engaged to him in order to annoy his horrible excuse for a father in exchange for him redoing my organization's website—oh, but he said he'd do that anyway, so I'm not really sure why I'm still pretending. And also? I want to jump his bones. For real, not for pretend.*

"She sent me an article on the computer. From November 29th! There were pictures of you with him. Were you ever going to tell me?"

It was impossible to miss the hurt in her mother's tone. Rosie had always imagined that if her mother somehow saw the *Gossip TO* post, which was extremely unlikely, she would tell her there had been a mistake, that the site was the internet equivalent of a tabloid. But she hadn't banked on

Marcus's aunt wading into the situation.

She did a quick mental cost-benefit analysis. Was it better to let her mother think she was really engaged but hadn't bothered to tell her? Or 'fess up to the great big lie?

"I was going to tell you."

Yep, she was gonna go with more lies. *Because that's always a good idea.* But she simply couldn't bear for her mother to think she was knowingly manipulating people. Deceiving them. She'd tell her the truth later, after it was all done.

"Is this the ring?"

Quadruple shitballs. Rosie had taken the ring off after her outing with Marcus earlier and left it on the counter. Which, at the time, she'd told herself was a stupid thing to do. But she'd been thinking more of thieves or, you know, accidental sink droppage. Not her mother. "It is."

"By the way, I'm taking the nine-thirty train home," said her mother, handing Rosie her coat.

What? Her mother always took the eight o'clock.

"We have a lot to talk about," she added. "Or rather, you have a lot to talk about."

"Okay," said Rosie, praying she could push back her date even later and ushering her mom into the dining room. "So, um, why did Marcus's aunt call?"

"She invited me to Hanukkah."

When Marcus arrived at the bar that night, all his assembled friends fell silent.

"What happened?" he asked, alarmed by their serious faces.

"What happened," said Dax's girlfriend Amy, "is that I got caught up this morning on some of my guilty pleasure websites, including *Gossip TO*."

And then they all erupted—except Lauren, who just sat there smirking. Marcus had a reputation for being remote at the office, he knew, so no one questioned the concept of him being engaged. It *wouldn't* be unlike him to be carrying on a secret romance and neglect to tell anyone—if he was the kind of person who went in for romance to begin with. So they bought the story. But they clearly were not going to allow the conversation to center on anything else all evening.

"You have to tell us more than that!" said Cassie, Jack's girlfriend, after Marcus tersely answered a few questions about Rose. "She works at this nonprofit, fine, but that's just her job. What's she *like*?"

"She's gorgeous," said Lauren, drawing everyone's attention. "She looks like Mindy Kaling with Bettie Page bangs."

"Oh my God, I *love* Mindy Kaling!" shrieked Amy. "She's basically the smartest, funniest, most stylish woman on the planet."

"Well, to be fair," said Lauren, "she's a lot taller than Mindy. And I've only met her once, but she was wearing the cutest—"

"Can we all stop discussing my fiancée as if we were at a horse auction?" snapped Marcus, genuinely annoyed.

"Whoa," said Amy, raising her hands in a surrendering gesture. "Point taken, but whoa."

"I think it's sweet," said Cassie, leaning against Jack, who was watching the whole exchange with obvious amusement, his barstool snug against his girlfriend's.

"So tell us something else about her," said Amy. "What

does she like to do for fun?"

"Does she like karaoke?" Cassie quipped. "I hope so, because she's gonna have trouble being in our girl gang if she doesn't."

"You can ask her yourself," said Dax, nodding toward the door. "Because if that isn't an Amazonian Mindy Kaling, I don't know who is."

What? Along with everyone else, Marcus turned to look at the front of the bar, and damned if his heart didn't speed up at the sight of her. She was wearing a pink coat—that must be the "non-crazy" one, but it was still a little out there. He wondered what color underwear she was wearing.

But then his brain dragged itself out of the gutter long enough to register the fact that she wasn't alone.

Of course, the tall, sport-coat-wearing guy with her had to be the classics professor, this week's Mr. Thursday Night. Except it was Saturday, which, according to Rose's own "rules," meant the date was somehow more serious. He watched Professor Smug guide her to a spot at the bar, help her onto the high stool. Watched Rose smile her thanks as she shrugged out of her coat to reveal a black and bright green striped cocktail dress, which probably meant she wasn't wearing the green underwear because Rose didn't do "matchy-matchy," to use her term. Watched Dr. Classics laugh at something she said, then open a menu and lay it out between them. Watched Rose lean in, snuggling right up next to him.

Like hell.

"Excuse me."

Whatever flare of boldness inspired Rosie to suggest Edward's—the bar Marcus explicitly told her he'd be at with his friends—when her date proposed they meet downtown extinguished itself the moment they stepped into the crowded restaurant. It was just that she'd been so angry at herself for playing this stupid engagement game. She was lying to everyone. She was lying to her *mother*, for God's sake, the woman who had dried her tears and given her nothing but encouragement for so many years.

And she was currently taking it out on Marcus. She was so mad at him for dragging her into his stupid charade. The idea of strolling in with her distinguished professor—charming, handsome, and kind, he was the most promising guy she'd met in months—and rubbing it in Marcus's face had been too tempting.

Except when she'd caught sight of him, sitting at a table on the other side of the bar, smiling and talking with his friends, she'd lost her nerve. Seeing him in his natural habitat, in this high-end bar surrounded by impossibly good-looking people, reminded her that, except insofar as it didn't jeopardize his twisted engagement prank, *Marcus didn't care who she dated.* So showing up thinking she was somehow taunting him only made her look pathetic.

Too proud to insist they change venues after she'd decided on this one, she led Kurt to a spot at the bar as far from Marcus's table as possible and sat with her back to it. When he opened a single menu between them, she seized the opportunity to lean into him a bit for some additional cover. Marcus wasn't expecting her, so maybe he wouldn't notice her.

"Rose. What a coincidence."

The voice came low and gravelly, right in her ear, and it unleashed a slow flood of warmth down her spine. It was an enormous relief, this warmth, as if she'd taken a drink of hot chocolate after coming in from the cold. She didn't like it. Didn't like that Marcus could just…make her feel relief. She was mad at him, she reminded herself. Really mad.

"Isn't it, though?" she said brightly—perhaps too brightly—and turned in place. God. He was wearing dark jeans and a fitted lavender button-down. And she wanted to eat him up. "Marcus, this is Kurt. Kurt, Marcus."

Kurt stuck out his hand but Marcus ignored it. "How do you two know each other?" her date asked.

Marcus stepped closer to her and raised his eyebrows, silently testing her with the idea that he might claim her as his fiancée. She had intended to come here to show him up, but she'd miscalculated, underestimated her opponent. She hadn't even been here five minutes and he had the upper hand, was utterly in control of the situation.

But she wasn't going to let him ruin her chances with Kurt. So she glared at him and tried to telegraph a command: *Don't you dare.*

"Rose is my—"

Shitballs! He was going to do it. She spoke over him, "Your aunt Rachel called my mother," and watched his eyes widen. Ha! See? She had her own conversational grenade. "She invited her to Hanukkah."

She waited for an expression of horror. But no, was he… laughing? It sure as hell looked like it. He was trying to muffle it, but there was no mistaking it. The bastard. She moved to turn back to the bar, but he blocked her with an arm. The absurd desire to reach out and feel his biceps unnerved her.

"We'll have to chat about Hanukkah later, since I'm here with Kurt." She physically moved his arm out of her way and smiled at the bewildered-looking professor. "I'm going to run to the ladies' room, Kurt. I'll be right back. It was nice running into you, Marcus."

There. Hopefully that would get rid of him.

It did not get rid of him. Five minutes later, when Rosie came out of the ladies' room, having touched up both her lipstick and her composure, she jumped about a foot to see Marcus *right there*.

So much for composure.

He took her arm silently and pulled her back into the shadows at the end of the corridor. "What the hell, Rose?"

"What the hell what?" she shot back. "I told you I wasn't going to stop going on dates."

"But you had to come *here*? Where you knew I would be."

Ha! Maybe she did have the power to ruffle his feathers a bit. She smirked. "Well, he wanted to meet somewhere in this area, and you were *just* saying how good this place was."

"You little minx." It went straight to her core, and she was instantly catapulted back to her sofa the night after her date with Dave. "People don't mock me and get away with it," he said, bending over and speaking into her ear while his hands rested on the wall on either side of her, caging her in.

"Did you know that Kurt is one of the world's foremost authorities on religious change in Roman Portugal?" she offered, still unable to get her voice to come out projecting the confidence she kept aiming for. In fact, it sounded embarrassingly shaky.

He didn't say anything right away, just cocked his head and looked at her.

And then he was kissing her. The distance that had been provided by his locked arms vanished in an instant, and there he was, all of him. Heat was pouring into her body from an unseen source as he anchored her head, one hand on each cheek, and feasted on her mouth. She sagged a little under the pure pleasure of the onslaught, and he somehow knew, because he inserted a thigh between hers, as if to help prop her up.

That thigh—it made things both better and worse. She gasped from the effort required not to grind herself against it, but that only seemed to spur him on—he pressed the leg more firmly against her, pivoting a little so she could feel the hardness of his erection against her hip.

Forget it. That did it. Knowing she was capable of having that kind of effect on him made her feel wild, just as it had at her apartment. Powerful. She abandoned all restraint and tightened her grasp on him—she had twined her arms around his neck before, but now she bent her elbows, hitching herself up against him as closely as possible and shamelessly wrapping one leg around him.

He groaned into her mouth and responded by letting his hands slide down from where he'd been palming her cheeks. They found their way to her ass, and the wicked leg that started this whole thing pressed even harder against her.

So she did the only sane thing she could do in that moment—she hitched her other leg around him, so that he was holding her against the wall with his body as she rode his thigh.

And the kiss kept going on and on, their tongues tangling, fighting for dominance. When she thought she couldn't possibly take it any more without having an orgasm then and there, he broke with her mouth, dragging his lips over her chin and down her throat.

Her head lolled back instinctively, to afford him better access, and as he hit the sensitive spot in the notch of her collarbone, she moaned.

"Oh, you like that, do you?" he said, then nipped the same spot with his teeth, which just about made her head explode as it triggered another, louder moan.

"Ahem."

Her head shot up. Kurt. "Oh my God," Rosie said, trying to push Marcus away as awareness and shame came flooding in.

He resisted, lifting his head from his evil ministrations to search her face. He must have seen her alarm because he looked over his shoulder and, with a muttered, "Shit," helped her slide down the wall.

Kurt cleared his throat. "You'd been gone a while, so I, ah, came back to look for you. You know what? I think I'm going to get going."

"Kurt, I'm so sorry. This isn't…" She trailed off. Despite the fact that this wasn't what Kurt thought, there really was no way to explain it. And no point in even trying because Kurt was already gone. Handsome, smart Kurt, her best prospect in months. *Years*.

"I'll take you home," Marcus said.

"Fuck off," she shot back, taking off down the corridor, lust alchemized into rage.

He was at her side in an instant. "Rose, if you think I'm just going to let you walk out of here alone at—"

"It's Toronto, Marcus," she snapped. "Not *A Nightmare on Elm Street*." As she made her way through the bar, Marcus close on her heels, she passed his friends' table, and they all erupted into speech. One of the women smiled and put her hand on Rosie's arm to interrupt her progress. That threw her for a bit of a loop. She was mad at Marcus, but she didn't want to seem like a freak in front of this group of very nice-looking strangers.

"Where has Marcus been hiding you?" said a dark-haired guy.

"When is the wedding?" called a blonde woman who seemed to be with the dark-haired guy.

"How do you put up with him?" asked the other man as he smirked.

"Everyone shut up," said the woman whose hand still rested on Rosie's arm. "You're overwhelming her." She smiled. "I'm Cassie."

"And I'm Amy," said the other woman. "There is one question that *must* be asked, though. Do you like karaoke?"

Rosie blinked under the assault, paralyzed. These people seemed so...nice. For an instant, she could imagine herself among them. At their table laughing, out for karaoke. Like she belonged with them because she belonged with Marcus.

There was that hand again, on her lower back, anchoring her just as she was about to let the barrage of questions tip her into panic mode. Goddamn him. There was no way Marcus should be able to make her feel better right now, much less with his *mere presence*. But there it was.

"Rose and I have had a bit of a mix-up, and we need

to hit the road," he said, smiling at his friends like it was nothing. Like he hadn't just ruined her date with Kurt and her chance for a boyfriend. Like he hadn't just nearly made her come, fully clothed, in the hallway outside the bathroom.

She knew when to admit defeat. She would let him drive her home. So she mustered what was left of her pride and smiled at the blonde woman. "I love karaoke."

Marcus knew Rose was angry. He had finally talked her into accepting a ride home. But when they got into the car and she didn't even bother greeting Nate before she raised the partition between the front and back seats, he realized exactly how much. She pivoted to face him, not even bothering to put on her seat belt. He braced for the worst, marshaling his arguments as to why Professor Dickhead wasn't right for her anyway.

"Hanukkah," she said.

He blinked. Shit. He had forgotten all about that little bomb she'd dropped on him at the bar. Making out with Rose had a way of making a man forget about everything except...well, about everything except his dick, to be crude about it. He sighed. Ruining her date was one thing. He was prepared to defend that. But ruining her relationship with her mother? Not so much. "I guess we should call it off."

"We can't call it off."

"Excuse me?" That was the last thing he expected her to say.

"We are going to Hanukkah, and we are putting on a show. The show of all shows. We're turning it up to eleven,

Marcus. Because this isn't just about your jerky dad anymore."

He shook his head, not understanding.

"I know it sounds weird, but I've given it a lot of thought. I had dinner with my mom, and I spent it convincing her that you were a good man."

"Thank you. I think," he said, trying to cover the strange, heavy feeling that settled in his chest when he thought of her describing him as a good man.

"She's even *excited* about Hanukkah. Apparently your aunt was really nice to her."

That he had trouble picturing. Rachel was his father's head cheerleader on the whole "Let's get Marcus to come back to the fold" project.

"I've given it a lot of thought. The lesser of two evils here is for me to string her along a little and tell her, sometime after Hanukkah, that we broke up."

"Really?" He had a bad feeling about all this. Because she was right. This wasn't just about his "jerky dad" anymore, to use her apt phrase. The stakes suddenly seemed much higher.

"Really. Because the alternative is for her to think I've been lying to her face all this time. And, Marcus, we don't do that in my family."

Aw, crap.

"So man up, Marcus. This shit just got real."

Chapter Ten

Marcus called Rose the next morning. He figured it was time to start making good on his side of their bargain beyond just the website. It was the least he could do now that his family dysfunction was spilling over and threatening her relationship with her mom. "Come to a cocktail party with me this afternoon at Leona van der Velde's house."

There was a beat of silence before she replied. "You mean Leona van der Velde, the chair of the EcoHabitat board?"

He grinned. "No, I mean the other Leona van der Velde." When he didn't get the laugh he'd been going for, he added, "She was a close friend of my mother's."

Rose made a strangled noise. "So she knows about the supposed engagement."

"Yes." There was no way to sugarcoat it. "She's having her annual Saint Nicholas party. She wants us to come."

"You go. You don't need me."

"Think strategically, Rose. This is a huge opportunity for you. She already knows I'm working on the website, so she'll ask about that. And she and her friends are rich as sin. You can tell them about the birds." After the sentence was out of his mouth, he noticed he hadn't said "birdies," in the mocking way he used to. "And this party is actually kind of fun. She's German, so she does it up. Flaming candles on the tree, the whole thing." He paused, delivering his fatal blow. "And, as a nod to the Saint Nick story, she gives all the women guests a pair of designer shoes as party favors."

There was a beat of silence, then: "What time should I be ready?"

Marcus surprised himself by actually looking forward to the van der Velde Christmas party. He hadn't been lying to Rose. As these things went, it was usually enjoyable. Probably because although Leona was a rich society wife—a lady who lunched—she wasn't of the Stepford variety. She reminded him of his mother that way. Leona was warm and fun and lacked the snobbishness so many in their social circle possessed. She kept the party small, and she did goofy, traditional things like force the guests to gather around the piano and sing carols.

This would be the first of Leona's parties without his mother. Last year, his mom had dolled herself up in a designer head scarf, painted on eyebrows, and asked him to escort her. He'd snuck her some eggnog—drinking was against the doctor's orders, but they'd both known it was going to be her last chance at Leona's famous homemade eggnog—and they'd whispered about the society gossip as they people-watched from a corner.

He knocked on Rose's door. He'd been dreading the party because this year, he wouldn't have his mother.

The door swung open.

But he would have Rose.

He drew in a breath. She always managed to wear something that was appropriate for the occasion and yet totally her—and by "totally her," he meant "totally off the wall." Today it was an emerald green cocktail dress. On the one hand, it was demure—it came to mid-calf and featured three-quarter length sleeves. But unlike many of the other dresses he'd seen her in, this one didn't flare at the hips. It hugged her curves—all of them—like a second skin. He let his eyes sweep down. And of course there were the hot pink heels. She must have been following his gaze because she said, "Yeah, I almost wore the red shoes, but then I thought that might be a little *too* Christmas-y."

The pink shoes were perfect. Perfectly wacky, but still perfect. "Damn, Rose, you're in the wrong business. You should be a stylist or something."

She brushed past him and hit the button for the elevator.

"Hey," he said, catching up with her and touching her arm. "That was a compliment."

She shook her head. "I'm sorry. I think I'm still mentally in middle school, where I was the opposite of stylish."

"Really?" It was hard to believe. "What were you like?"

"Well, to start with, I shot up to this height in eighth grade, so I towered over everyone, even the boys."

"Everyone's awkward at that age."

"Well, Tiffany and Ashley, aka my tormenters, were not

awkward."

Thinking of a young Rose, who had not yet grown into her confidence and beauty, suffering, made him want to find these Tiffany and Ashley people and make them rue the day they decided to mess with Rose Verma.

She paused for a moment before stepping into the lobby, thoughtful. "In some ways, I brought it on myself. I could have traded in my combat boots for their Keds, worn my skirts skankily short, styled my hair like them, but...I don't know. Conforming to their norms felt like giving in somehow."

He tamped down his anger. Rose didn't need him going vigilante on her bullies. She'd faced them just fine. "You were always yourself, Rose Verma."

"Whatever." She climbed into the car and smiled, seeming to shake off the heavy mood that had settled over her. "Hi, Nate!"

It looks like Saint Nicholas has brought you a little something, my dear!" Leona van der Velde thrust a shoe into Rosie's hand after enveloping her in a bear hug.

In her mind, Rosie knew she was making another foray into Marcus's gilded, old-money world. She thought she was prepared, was aiming to be a little less dumbstruck than she had been at the Fall Ball.

But somehow, Rosie was still surprised when Leona handed her a black Christian Louboutin pump filled with Godiva chocolates. Marcus had compared his social world to *Gossip Girl*, but if she'd seen this on that show, she would have scoffed.

"Before you leave, run upstairs to the shoe room and either find its mate or, if it's not your size or to your taste, swap it for one of the extra pairs on the shelves. I try to match each guest to a pair of shoes that suits them, but since we haven't had the pleasure of getting to know each other, I had to play it a little safe with my selection for you.

"And you!" It was Marcus's turn for the bear hug. "I miss your mom something fierce."

When she pulled back, she had tears in her eyes. Rosie snuck a glance at Marcus. He swallowed. "Me, too, Leona. Me, too."

"Come in, come in!" She took Rosie's arm. "Now, I know we've met in passing at EcoHabitat." It was true. After Leona took over for Marcus's mom as chair of the board, she had taken a tour of the office and been introduced to all the staff. "But if I had known you were Marcus's intended bride—my goodness, I would have paid a great deal more attention!"

The party was a whirlwind. Leona introduced Rosie to a trio of women, one of whom was an active supporter of forest conservation. "She's into trees, and she's rich as sin," Leona whispered in Rosie's ear. "Be charming, and I'll shake her down for EcoHabitat later." Then she raised her voice. "Rose is also Marcus Rosemann's fiancée! Take care of her while I go greet some other guests, won't you, ladies?"

That got their attention. "How ever did you manage that?" said one of them, looking Rosie up and down without even trying to be subtle about it.

Rosie scanned the room for Marcus, hoping to catch his eye and somehow will him to come rescue her. But he appeared to be similarly cornered, surrounded by a group of younger, beautiful women.

Marcus's girls.

She turned back to the ladies who lunch.

"Will you take Marcus's last name, dear?" said one of them. "Normally, I would think so—you're marrying into one of Toronto's best families, after all. But won't Rose Rosemann be a tad awkward?"

Marcus had just made his escape from Leona's daughter and her friends and had been intending to rescue Rose from the clutches of a group of Leona's contemporaries, when the hammer came down.

And by "hammer," he meant "Gail."

His jaw locked as it always did when he saw his…what? What was she? He could hardly call her his ex. They'd gone on maybe three dates in college, and that was twenty years ago now. Family friend? Her family and his went way back, their grandparents having all been members of the same downtown synagogue before subsequent generations decamped for the suburbs.

"Marcus," she said in that fake purr of hers. "How's the Magnifique campaign coming? Ready for the pitch next week?"

Right. *Nemesis* was the word he was looking for.

Gail had never stopped trying to one-up him after he broke up with her. But you could hardly even call it breaking up since they'd only gone on three dates. Regardless, she'd spent the last two decades working her way up through the

Toronto advertising world, and she was always trying to show him up. She was good—he had to give her that. The campaigns that came out of the firm she'd just made partner at were always solid, sometimes brilliant. He admired them the way he admired any smart ad. Healthy competition was good.

But that was the problem—it wasn't *healthy* competition with her. She made everything into a production, as if she were forever trying to get back at him.

He had to unclench his teeth to say, "Fine, Gail."

"You gonna tell me any of your secrets? Give me a little hint?" She ran her hand up and down his lapel. Why the hell did she always do that?

As always, he had to prevent himself from physically shaking her off. "What do you think?"

But she wasn't really paying attention all of a sudden, was absorbed by something over his shoulder. Before he could twist around to see what it was, she put her hands on his shoulders, lifted herself onto her tiptoes and brushed a kiss across his chin—it was as high as she could reach. He tried to step back, but she threw her arms around his neck and whispered in his ear, "That was just a little kiss for luck, Marcus. Because you're going to need it."

God, she was like the wicked witch from a fairy tale, a caricature villain.

He wormed his way out of her grasp, but then she stuck her hand in his face. "Would you rather kiss my hand? That seems to be your thing, doesn't it?"

What? Then, with a thud, it hit him. "You're the one who tipped off *Gossip TO*."

Her features arranged themselves into a parody of confusion as she snatched her hand back. "What do you mean?"

"How do you know about the hand kissing?"

Her eyes flicked to the side and then back. "I saw the pictures like everyone else."

"No, you *took* the pictures." It was hard to say why, but he just knew. Gail was always doing things to get his goat. It never made any sense, but he had learned that trying to apply logic to Gail was a fruitless exercise.

"I'm sure I don't spend nearly as much time thinking about you and your little girlfriend as you seem to think I do, Marcus."

Forget it. It didn't matter anyway. He was done expending emotional energy on Gail. Without a word, he turned around, intending to walk away. His gaze immediately found Rose's face.

Rose's very pissed off face.

"There she goes again," said one of the ladies who lunch.

Rosie and the other women gathered in their little group followed the first woman's gaze—to where that Gail chick, who was looking very elegant in a cream pantsuit—was fondling Marcus.

"Have you met Gail?" said Leona Friend #1.

"Of course, she's met Gail," said Leona Friend #2. "The Rosemanns and the Abrams go way back. They're practically family."

"They *would* have been family if Marcus's mother had had her way."

"What do you mean?" Rosie said, wary, not sure she

wanted to know the answer, but unable to stop herself from asking.

"Oh, she fixed them up years ago. It didn't work out."

Gail was exactly the sort of woman Marcus should marry. Beautiful, from the same old-money world, professionally accomplished in the same industry as Marcus. And Jewish to boot.

"I have met Gail," said Rosie, a little too loudly, but she didn't care. "It's been lovely chatting with you all, but if you'll excuse me."

I need to go have a word with my fake fiancé.

Because this Gail shit isn't going to fly.

"**M**ay I speak with you, please?"

"Of course. I was just coming to find you. There are a bunch of people here who might be interested in the wetland…"

She turned and headed for the stairs in the middle of his sentence.

Oh, man, Rose was mad. He could tell by the way she carried herself, all stiff and extra upright. He followed, avoiding eye contact with partygoers as they made their way through the living room. As Rose passed Leona, she held up her shoe and said, in a singsong voice he clearly recognized as a mask for how pissed she was, "Can't resist making a visit to the shoe room! Be right back!"

"I'm sorry I left you for so long, but those women you were with are good people to know if—*ouf.*" She yanked him inside a room at the top of the stairs, shut the door behind them, pressed him up against it, and promptly began making out with him. It took his body a second to catch up—but only a second. He grabbed her waist and pulled her more firmly against him as she shoved her tongue into his mouth, causing a bolt of lightning to spike up his spine.

"Remember when you said you could talk while you kissed?" she breathed, pulling away just long enough to get the question out before she was back nipping his lips.

"Mmmm-hmmm."

"So what the hell was that with Gail? All those women out there are talking about how you used to date her."

He'd been trying to shut her up with his mouth, but she was determined to talk—and of course, he was the one who had started the whole talking-while-kissing thing. So he switched tactics. "That was nothing," he rasped, dragging his lips down her throat to her chest. He didn't tease, he just went straight for the impressive cleavage her dress was displaying and pressed his mouth against it, letting his senses fill with her—her herbal scent, her soft skin.

"Unnnhh," she moaned, but then her hands came to his head—one on each side—and she yanked it back up and glared at him. "You're fake engaged to *me*, Marcus. *Me*. Have a little respect."

She was getting a taste of her own medicine—now she knew what he felt like dog-sitting while she went on her Thursday night dates or watching her canoodle with the world's foremost expert on religious change in Roman Portugal. He might have laughed if he hadn't been so turned on. "I do respect you," he muttered as he ran his hands up and down her dress, trying to find a zipper or some other means of removal. "Gail was being her usual melodramatic self, and…" He hesitated, not sure how she would take the news.

"And?"

"I'm pretty sure she's the one who sold us out to *Gossip TO.*"

"Oh my God. What are we going to—"

He gave up on the dress and pulled her down to the floor with him.

She came right with him, Gail apparently forgotten, allowing herself to be maneuvered so she was lying on top of him. My God, she felt good, her soft curves settling against him like her body was made for him. She sighed and lowered her head to kiss him again, softer this time, slower. He groaned when she opened her mouth, granting him entrance, and each little whimper she made ramped up the invisible pressure on his cock, which she wasn't even touching.

Until—"Oh, God!" he bit out—she was. Her hand had snaked down, and she stroked him through his pants.

This could not continue. Not here. So he grabbed her and rolled them over, intending to position himself on top so he could better control things—in other words, keep it going but also not embarrass himself.

Instead, he rolled them over so they crashed into the bottom of the three-layer shelf that ringed the room, full of high heels.

Which came raining down on them.

Rose shrieked as Marcus shielded her from the falling stilettos.

And then they both burst out laughing.

"Oh my God, what are we doing?" Rose scrambled to her feet and started gathering shoes. "Anyone could have walked in on us."

He started helping her, trying to match up pairs. "Hey," he said, holding up a yellow patent leather number. "Maybe you should trade in yours for this."

She glanced over, and he could see the desire take root in her eyes. He was stupidly proud that her shoe-lust look wasn't as intense as her regular-lust look had been a moment ago. "Find me that in a size nine, and I'll be your best friend for life."

He started scanning the room.

"A-ha!" she said, lifting a pair of the yellow pumps over her head. "Victory."

"Hang on," he said, smoothing her hair, which they'd managed to mess up pretty spectacularly.

Rolling her eyes, she endured his ministrations. When he was done, she turned to go, but he caught her arm. "One more thing," he said, as he hauled her back, circling his arms around her so her back was flush with his front. He leaned down to whisper in her ear. "I swear to God, Rose, one of these days we are going to finish this."

Chapter Eleven

Marcus was off his game at a run-through for the Magnifique pitch later that week. They had some solid mock-ups and the concept was as good as it was going to get—and he was confident that it was objectively *good*—so all that remained was to hone the presentation itself.

Which was on him.

And he was *not* delivering.

The problem was he couldn't stop thinking about how he had practically mauled his fake fiancée in a pile of shoes at a high society party over the weekend. And he'd spent so much time hanging out with Rose in recent days that the concepts weren't second nature to him like they should have been.

"Why don't we just take it again from the top?" said Lauren, who was standing next to him at the head of the table in the conference room filled with their senior people, just as she would be doing when the two of them gave the actual presentation.

"Right," he said. The problem was that every time he started talking about lipstick, he started thinking about lips. Rose's lips, to be precise. Painted red or magenta or some other obnoxiously unnatural hue.

Rose's lips parting under his.

Or falling open on a moan as she ground herself against his thigh.

And there he went again.

The irony was not lost on him. He was trying to sell lipstick, but he was too distracted by…lips to be any good at it.

"You know what?" he said, after ten seconds of silence while everyone stared at him with expressions ranging from slightly bewildered to totally gobsmacked. "Let's take ten."

"What the hell is the matter with you?" Lauren whispered, pulling him into a corner as the rest of the room's inhabitants either headed for the coffee machine or broke into smaller conversations. "Take a breath."

"I am."

"Then take another one, and get your goddamned act together. We have five days, Marcus. *Five days*. Which really means four because you're off for Hanukkah the night before the pitch."

She didn't need to tell him how important this was. That was one of the great things about Lauren. She wasn't going to stand for shit when the stakes were this high.

"If you can't do this, just tell me, and we'll switch. I'll take the lead, and you can be Vanna White for once."

"I just need a minute—and a cup of coffee." His phone rang. It was her. "I've got to take this." He didn't even wait until he was sure he was out of earshot before picking up the call. "Rose?"

"Marcus. I need help."

There was a hint of desperation in her tone. Like she was trying to keep her voice even but not quite succeeding. His stomach dropped as he strode into the corridor and toward his office. "What's wrong? Where are you?"

"I'm fine. I'm just in a bit of a bind, and I…don't have anyone else I can ask."

"Tell me." This wasn't like her. "Where are you? I'll come get you."

"What are you doing right now? Can I meet you at your house?"

He was about to insist on coming to her, wherever she was, when she added, "You do live in a house, right? Not, like, the penthouse at the Ritz?"

He wasn't sure if that was supposed to be a joke. "Uh, no, I live in a house. In Yorkville."

"Can I meet you there?"

"Why won't you let me come get you?" *Why won't you tell me what's wrong?*

"Trust me. I'll come to you."

Sighing, he rattled off his address, hung up, and headed back to the conference room. "Something's come up," he said to Lauren, ignoring her dropped jaw.

"You can't just bail on us now."

There was a first time for everything.

"Same time tomorrow," he said over his shoulder. "And I promise I'll have it together."

Fifteen minutes later, Marcus was sitting on his porch fretting. Rose was usually so composed. So self-contained. From the sounds of it, she was well-practiced in standing up to bullies. It was hard to imagine her needing to ask anyone for help. So of course his imagination was conjuring all sorts of worrisome scenarios. Had someone died? He realized they'd talked at great length about his family, but he had never asked about hers. She'd mentioned her mother, and he knew her father was dead, but who else was there? What kind of a jerk was he that he had no idea?

Or maybe it wasn't that at all. Had she lost her job? Though she might be upset by that, he would see it as no great loss. From what he could tell, despite her title as manager of fundraising, Rose pretty much ran EcoHabitat.

There was no point in speculating, the rational part of his mind knew, but it was almost impossible to stop. He got up and walked down the path to the sidewalk. His house was only a ten minute walk from the Bay subway station, so regardless of whether she was coming from home or from work, she should have arrived by now.

Unless she'd walked the whole way.

With an enormous black dog.

One that was barking its head off. In fact, he heard them before they appeared from around the corner at the end of his street. She was walking a huge rottweiler on a leash—or maybe it was more accurate to say that a huge rottweiler on a leash was walking her.

"Marcus!" she called, and he jogged down the sidewalk to meet her, which caused the dog to lose its mind.

"Salt!" she hollered. "Sit!" Only Rose would name a huge black dog Salt.

The entreaty only caused the mutt to grow more agitated.

"Hi," said Rose, flashing Marcus a small smile as he took the leash from her.

"Shut up," Marcus commanded the dog, who, mysteriously, obeyed. It even sat down for good measure and looked up at him, panting.

"Whoa!" Rose exclaimed. "See? She already likes you!"

What did she mean by "already?" *Oh, no. No, no, no.*

"It turns out my building has these ridiculous breed bans. No rottweilers or pit bulls, and—"

This was why he'd bailed on the Magnifique run-through? "No way, Rose."

"I didn't know about the ban when I agreed to take her. One of my neighbors ratted me out, and—"

This was not happening. "I don't know why you keep talking because I am no longer listening."

"All my friends live in condos or apartments! The only person I know who has a yard is my mother, and she's not up to the task."

"I'm not doing it."

"Marcus," she said, finally stopping the endless torrent of talking and looking up at him with big, watery brown eyes. "They were going to kill her. Her owners brought her to the shelter to be put down because they were moving and couldn't be bothered with her anymore."

He closed his eyes for a moment to shut out the sight of her. When he opened them again, he noticed that everything about her was different than usual. Her lips were bare, which was unprecedented. In fact, she had no makeup on, her hair was pulled back into a ponytail, and she was wearing sweatpants. It was like Rose's schleppy twin had come instead of her. But, strangely, the effect was not any less potent than Dressed to the Nines Rose. She was still gorgeous.

"Just for a few days?" she whispered, suddenly sounding defeated. Like she'd known he would say no. Then she added a tentative, "Please?"

He heaved an enormous sigh, which caused her to jump up and down in glee—and which, in turn, caused Salt to succumb to another fit of barking.

"Knock it off," he snarled at the pooch.

Salt knocked it off.

"Oh, wow," said Rose, "you *really* have a way with her."

He glared at her.

"Okay," she said, "I'm going to go out and buy the supplies you'll need, and I'll be right back. If you can just—"

"Come in," he interrupted. "I'll send Nate out."

"But you shouldn't have to pay for—"

"Come in," he said again, more forcefully. He had to bite his tongue to stop himself from adding, "We have unfinished business." But if he'd left what was arguably the most important meeting of the quarter to meet Rose, he suddenly felt like making sure at least *some* loose ends finally got tied up. Knowing that Rose was looking for a real boyfriend, he should probably do the honorable thing and leave her alone. But he simply couldn't stand it anymore.

When she just kept standing there like a deer in headlights, he took her elbow with one hand and tightened his grip on Salt's leash with the other. "I bailed on a big meeting to meet you here, and I'm taking your goddamned dog, so the least you can do is come inside for five minutes."

Instead of leading her up the porch, Marcus headed around to the back of the house to find Nate. The chauffeur had driven him home from the office and, unsure what was going on with Rose, Marcus had instructed him to wait.

"I need you to run an errand," Marcus said. "I am, apparently"—he shot a look at Rose—"the temporary guardian of this beast. I need you to go to a pet store and get whatever she'll need. Just tell them she's a rottweiler." He looked at Rose. "Do you know how old she is?"

"The shelter said they thought two or three."

He nodded at Nate. "So just get whatever they tell you to get."

"All she needs is food," Rose protested, digging in her purse. "Don't let them sell you all kinds of stuff you don't—"

Marcus reached out to physically block her from extracting her wallet. "Get whatever they tell you to get," he said.

Rose rolled her eyes as Nate got into the car. But as her head tilted up in the process, it stopped and didn't come back down. "Are those *solar* panels?"

He followed her gaze up to the roof. "They are."

"Oh my God, how long have you had them?" She clutched his arm. "What's your estimate of how long they're going to take to pay for themselves? Do you ever end up feeding the grid?"

"I've had them for three years. Probably seven or eight more until I recoup my investment. And as for your last question, nope, I have to supplement with regular electricity." He pointed to the huge oak tree in the yard. "There's too much tree coverage here—it blocks the sun."

She clasped her hands together under her chin, looking up in wonderment. He had a lot of cool stuff in his house. Historically, he had made an impression on women with his indoor lap pool, his home theater system, or his giant soaker bathtub. But he had a feeling that this particular woman was going to be most impressed by a bunch of ugly-ass panels on the top of his roof.

"Come on, let's go inside."

Marcus's house was like a spread in *Architectural Digest*. Like his suits, or that sofa in his office she'd been so entranced by, everything was impeccable and understated but made from the finest material. The casual sitting area he led them through as they came in the patio door was one of those rooms that just made you feel like settling in for the long haul. A huge, overstuffed sofa was angled so anyone lounging on it could see the backyard through the wall of glass that was the back of the house. And the table in front of it was littered with newspapers. Rosie could imagine waking up and spending a lazy Saturday morning in here with coffee, bagels, and the news.

No, she could imagine *Marcus* doing that. Because she did not live here, she reminded herself.

They moved into a kitchen that literally made her jaw drop. As Marcus got out a bowl and filled it with water for Salt, she took in immaculate stainless steel appliances, an enormous island topped in a single slab of marble that had to be twelve feet long, and the sweetest little breakfast nook that was a booth tucked under some slanted walls. Between it and that sitting room, she could move right in and happily exist in only these two rooms for the rest of her life. In fact, she was so tired and cold from her hours outside without proper winter wear that she had to fight the impulse to crawl over to that nook right now and fall asleep on one of those benches. "Marcus, this place is off the hook."

He grinned as he bent to place Salt's bowl on the floor, then loosened his tie as he stood back up, which, embarrassingly, caused her to catch her breath a little. "And here I thought it was all going to be downhill in your eyes after you saw the solar panels."

"Can I see the rest of the house?"

"Of course."

As he took her through perfectly appointed room after perfectly appointed room, starting with the finished basement, which housed a guest suite, a small lap pool, and a home theater, she started to really understand why she was a problem in Marcus's father's eyes. Clearly, Marcus was far, far richer than she had understood. He had a pool *in his house*, for God's sake. If this was normal to him, she was definitely the girl from the wrong side of the tracks. She was so far over the tracks that they didn't even live in the same town.

"Is she going to be okay by herself if we go upstairs?" Marcus glanced down at Salt as they paused at the base of the stairs to the second floor. The dog had magically ceased her barking once they were inside Marcus's house and had been silently trailing them on the tour.

He looked so adorably baffled. He really hadn't been kidding, apparently, when he said he wasn't an animal person. "She's a rottweiler. Of course she'll be okay."

They started up—but so did Salt.

"It probably is better if you keep her down there," said Rosie, eyeballing the very expensive-looking Persian-style carpet runner lining the stairs. "I mean, I'm sure she's house trained, but…" She turned to the dog and pointed back down the stairs. "Stay."

Salt just panted and took another step up.

"Stay," said Marcus, repeating her directive in a firm voice that not only caused Salt to turn tail and go back to the landing, but caused Rosie to shiver a little.

"Damn, Marcus," she said. "It's like you're the Dog Whisperer."

"Why don't you have any makeup on?" he asked as he led the way upstairs.

"What?" It took her a moment to catch up to the sudden change of subject. "Oh, because I took Salt for a walk early this morning, and when I got back to my building, someone from the condo board was waiting for me, waving these *by-laws*"—she made air quotes with her fingers—"and insisting that I couldn't come back into the building with her. They wouldn't even let me go upstairs and make myself present-able for a day spent trying to find foster care for a hundred-pound rottweiler."

"What *have* you been doing all day?" He looked at his watch as he waited for her at the top of the stairs. "It's nearly three o'clock."

She sighed. The question drew her attention to her aching feet. "What I have been doing all day is schlepping that mutt around trying to find a shelter spot in this godforsaken city."

"On foot?"

"Judging by the state of my aching feet, that would be a yes. Some public transit, but mostly walking."

"What about work?"

"I called in sick. I literally had nowhere to put Salt. I figured, it's not like if I'm not at that office for one day, the whole place will fall apart."

He smiled at her—a smile that warmed her still-cold insides. She'd warmed up somewhat now that they were in the house, but her extremities were still freezing. "That place probably *will* fall apart without you. From my admittedly limited vantage point, it seems like you do everything there."

Maybe it was the exhaustion, but that felt like the nicest thing anyone had ever said to her. "So this is your office?" she said, since she wasn't sure how to respond to his remark about her role at work. He'd led her to a room dominated by a large mid-century teak desk covered with papers and books—and three computers. That was the thing about Marcus's house. It was gorgeous and classy and tasteful and all that, but it also looked like he actually *lived* in it. Like the magazine people showed up a day earlier than scheduled to photograph it.

"You should ask for a promotion."

"I know," she said. "I admit I'm not good at advocating for myself. But in this case, I also know that the answer will be no."

"Guest room," he said, opening the door to a room that looked like something out of a fancy hotel and, unlike the rest of the house, appeared untouched. "Why don't you move on from EcoHabitat?"

She sighed. "I know you think I'm a total hippie wingnut vegetarian, but I'm really not. I just think we have to do better on a lot of fronts, and EcoHabitat's idea about finding better ways for humans and ecosystems to coexist seems like a reasonable, doable thing, if we can only keep amassing support."

They'd peeped into a TV room and a bathroom and

were poised at the bottom of another set of stairs when he said, "I don't think you're a wingnut."

Salt, of course, chose that moment to bark from the first floor.

He grinned. "Well, maybe not a *total* wingnut. Your devotion to the cause is admirable. I just hate that the side effect is that you end up selling yourself short."

Another bark. "Can it, Salt!" Marcus bellowed.

Salt canned it. Naturally.

"What's up here?" She gestured up the stairs.

"Up there is my lair."

She burst out laughing. "Your *lair*? What are you, Batman?" The phrase *Marcus's girls* popped into her head, though, and her laughter died on her lips. Maybe it was more of a Hugh Hefner-style lair. She took a step back.

"Come on." He took her hand in his. "You're freezing," he said, and it was true. His hand felt like a big, warm mitten enveloping hers.

She wanted to blurt out that he was welcome to warm her up. But that was probably something one of Marcus's girls would say. And in her *au naturel* state, she looked like the "before" picture from a makeover.

The stairs opened up into a loft-style space that spanned the whole top floor of the house. There was an enormous bed in the center of the room, covered with a simple but luxurious-looking white duvet. The front was taken up by one of those bathrooms that didn't have a wall—the kind that always seemed wildly impractical when she saw them in magazines. The hardwood of the bedroom floor gave way to tiny glass tiles that sparkled in various shades of blue. They sloped downward toward an enormous claw-footed soaker tub and a shower area that had one wall of glass to demarcate it but was otherwise open.

She pivoted to face the third section of the room, a little sitting area that faced the back of the house. As with the main floor, the back wall had been blown out and replaced with glass. That, together with several skylights, gave the impression that they were in a tree house. "Oh!" she exclaimed, walking toward the glass. They were surrounded by trees, but they had shed their leaves for the season. "I bet this is even more beautiful in the summer."

She mentally revised her previous thought. Instead of spending her whole life in the kitchen-sunroom combination on the main floor, she'd spend it here, thank you very much. "How can your father not be impressed by all this?" she said without thinking. Because if she had, she wouldn't have brought up his father.

"We didn't come up here to talk about my father."

Fair enough. She was about to reluctantly peel her attention from the yard when he added, "We came up here because we have unfinished business."

I swear to God, one of these days we are going to finish this. The last sentence he'd spoken to her last time she saw him began ricocheting around in her chest, which was suddenly empty of air.

She was frozen, like an ice statue, unable to get a purchase on anything: breath, rational thought, warmth.

Suddenly he was behind her, crowding her. Just like at the bar Saturday night, but this time she was facing away from him, looking out over his stunning backyard.

She knew what was coming next.

Yes. There it was—that voice, low in her ear. Even

though there was no one around this time and so no need to whisper. And with it came the warmth his hand at her back always brought, which was so, so welcome. His breath huffed against her neck. "I'm sick of this little dance we're doing."

What was he talking about? Was he calling off the fake engagement before Hanukkah? And why was the prospect so disappointing?

"I think we should just call this thing between us what it is."

"What is it?" Her voice came out more confident than she felt. She sounded almost like she was challenging him.

"Lust."

She inhaled sharply. Suddenly the warmth was replaced by heat. It didn't flood in like it had last time. It was just there. Everywhere. Prickling her skin, beating a pulse between her legs, making her face flush. She pressed her palms against the glass of the wall, suddenly feeling like the room was tilting, and there was nothing to hold onto.

Though he hadn't said any more, his mouth still hovered next to her ear. He had to be able to see the insane thrumming of her pulse at her throat. They stayed like that for a long moment while a coil wound itself up in the few inches of space between them, drawing the tension ever tighter, making her already ragged breath shorter. Then his hands were on hers, pressing against the backs of her palms and sliding them higher up the glass until her arms were fully extended above her head.

She wanted more than anything for him to press himself against her, to feel the powerful erection he never tried to hide. Each second that he didn't touch her was an exquisite torture. Finally, he spoke again. "I thought it was all those crazy colors. Those magenta lips, rainbow colored dresses, and fuck-me shoes."

She looked down at her ratty gray sweats as he spoke. They were about as far as it was possible to get from her usual look.

"But it wasn't," he rasped, his voice almost impossibly deep. "I need you to know two things. The first is that I want to make absolutely clear you understand that I don't do relationships."

"And the second?" she asked, breathless.

"The second is that right now, I want to be inside you more than I've ever wanted anything."

She moaned. She couldn't help it. No one had ever spoken to her this way, and it turned out that it had been exactly what was missing.

She waited, hoping he would say more. Do more.

But of course, that was Marcus for you. He'd stated his case, and now he was leaving it up to her. He was probably the only guy on the planet who was capable of being gentlemanly while talking dirty.

All right. It wasn't like she was indecisive about this. He wasn't one of her Mr. Thursday Night candidates, but who the hell cared? As he'd said multiple times, he didn't do relationships. And she was young and single. And, more than likely, in a few weeks, her mother would set her up with some nice, inoffensive doctor she could almost guarantee was never going to push her up against a glass wall and whisper filthy things in her ear.

So, leaving her left hand where it was, she tugged on her right one, which caused him to release it. Yes, she looked awful right now. But she'd meant what she said earlier when she'd told him she wore the fancy undies for herself. Without turning around, she forced her clumsy fingers to grasp the zipper of her hoodie. Slowly, trying to draw out the moment in the hopes that he was feeling a fraction of the torture she was, she pulled down the zipper, the scratch of the teeth coming apart deafening in the otherwise silent room. When she was done, she shrugged her right arm out, which left her left arm, still pinned to the wall, in its sleeve while the rest of the hoodie dangled.

"Fuck," he groaned, and power surged inside her. She was wearing a bright yellow bra with black polka dots. It had cracked her up when she bought it, reminding her of the "Itsy Bitsy Teenie Weenie" song. But now it seemed dead serious. And suddenly it was imperative that she show him the matching bottom. He still had her left hand pinned to the glass, and when she resisted, he didn't let her go like he had on the other side. He just stood there behind her, radiating heat.

"Marcus," she breathed as she tried to free her hand. Speaking was as difficult as if she had just run a race. "I want to take off my pants." When he still didn't move, she added, "You need to let go of me."

"That is not a good idea," he growled.

It seemed like the best idea in the world to her. She had managed to pull the waistband of her sweatpants off her hips with her free hand, but with her body stretched out, she couldn't reach any farther, or bend at the waist to aid her own efforts. It amazed her that she had ever been cold in her whole life, much less mere minutes ago, because she was sweltering in these pants. Suffocating. "Why not?" she said, writhing her hips futilely in an attempt to get the damned pants off.

"Because if you take those pants off now, frankly, I'm going to have to fuck you like this, right against this wall. And I'm going to last about ten seconds."

She screamed a little then, turning her head to muffle it with her shoulder. It was partly frustration, but mostly all-consuming, full body want. "Do it," she said, looking over her shoulder for the first time to meet his gaze. She would have expected him to be looking at her body, but the blue-gray gaze found her eyes the moment she turned. She wanted to throw her head back and laugh, half in triumph, half in glee, to see the struggle for control written so plainly across his face. Eyes glazed, brow furrowed, the vein she'd seen pop when his father got to him looked like it wanted to jump out of his skin. "Do it," she said again, whispering this time because her throat had dried up. "Marcus, please."

It was like an old-fashioned VHS tape: the scene paused for a moment, each of them staring at the other. But it was as if only the external action paused. She was painfully aware of every sensation inside her body: the blood pounding between her legs, nipples tightened to almost painful peaks, knees shaking.

Pause gave way to fast forward then, and she almost cried out at the loss of sensation as he left her—which was ridiculous because the only place he'd been touching her was where their joined hands pressed against the window. She craned her neck around to see him tossing aside a condom wrapper. She felt a momentary twinge of regret that she'd suggested—no, insisted—that they do it this way. Because she wanted to see him. All of him.

"Ah!" she gasped as he shoved down her panties and

dragged a finger across her. Under other circumstances, she might have been embarrassed at how wet she was. But in this case, she hoped he would interpret it as a sign that he should hurry. He'd said he wasn't going to last, but neither was she. Her clit was throbbing so hard she had to press her palm against it. She wasn't sure if her aim was to make herself come or to stop herself from coming too soon. It didn't matter, though, because there was no way to not touch herself.

It was a shock when her hand was shoved roughly aside. "That's my job," he snarled. She gasped, and then cried out when the fingers of his right hand burrowed through her folds while the other hand guided his penis inside her. "Okay?" he whispered when he was buried to the hilt.

Beyond words, she nodded vigorously, hoping he would interpret the inhuman moan that ripped from her throat as assent. But oh, it had been a while. The feeling of fullness, of stretching, of giving and receiving pleasure. It was a drug. And, even though they were less than five seconds into it, she was certain she'd never had a lover as good as Marcus. He must be decoding the animalistic sounds she was making correctly because he established a rhythm immediately. He would pull out slowly—agonizingly so—and then pause for a beat before unceremoniously slamming back into her. And it was so, so good. Each thrust pressed her harder against the glass—and against his arm, because it was wedged between her and the wall, his fingers expertly teasing and circling her clit, sending her spiraling higher and higher.

Then he started talking. One phrase at the end of each thrust. "You little tart," was the first. She arched her back and shamelessly ground herself against his fingers as if to prove his point. "You're going to make me come in about five seconds," was the second, and it made her whole body vibrate. "And you'd better damn well be planning to come with me," he rasped the third time. It was enough—it was more than enough—to send her over the edge. As the waves of pleasure radiated out from her core, he thrust a few more times, each one harder than the last until he gave a great cry and stayed buried in her, pressing his entire body along the length of hers and shuddering violently.

They stayed like that for a long while. Probably this was the part where embarrassment should begin creeping in— she'd just begged to be taken up against a window, for God's sake. But she couldn't muster any. There was too much bone-deep satiation for there to be room for anything else. When he pulled away, she wanted to cry out her objection. Even though it was obviously impossible, she wished she could stand here with him forever, in this room in the treetops. She could hear him dealing with the condom, and she laid her forehead on the glass, spent.

With a mighty effort and a deep sigh, she finally turned, intending to gather up her gross sweats and get dressed— only to find him in the process of undressing. Huh? She must have looked as confused as she felt because he shot her a wicked grin and crooked his finger at her. She took a step toward him, and he took a step back. They repeated the same sequence two more times. Each time he shed a little more of his clothing.

"What are you doing?" she finally said.

"That happened too damned fast. I didn't even get my clothes off, which, in retrospect, seems like a huge lost opportunity."

She wasn't sure she agreed. There had been something

intensely erotic about feeling his clothed body against her bare skin, his suit soft and scratchy at the same time.

"Take off your bra," he said. After what they'd just done, the command should not have shocked her. But it did. Because even though he'd been stripping and beckoning her toward the bed, she somehow hadn't put together that he was gunning for an encore. She…wasn't sure how she felt about that. On the one hand: yeessss! But somehow, having wild, animalistic sex against the wall with a fully clothed Marcus Rosemann one time seemed like an impulsive aberration. Having sex with a naked Marcus Rosemann in his bed five minutes after having had wild, animalistic sex against the wall with a fully clothed Marcus Rosemann seemed…ill-advised. Because lust aside, she and Marcus were not on the same page at all when it came to relationships.

She'd hesitated too long, though, because now he was fully naked, standing before her unflinchingly. And was he a fifteen-year-old inside the body of a forty-year-old, because—hello!—he was at attention again. She wanted to look more closely, to touch.

Oh, God, she wanted to taste.

So she took off her bra.

Well, she'd wanted to see him before, and now she was getting her wish. So she forced her eyes upward. Not only was the man a millionaire CEO, he was also apparently a Greek god. Every part of him was sleek and muscular but not bulky, as if he had put in more than his share of hours in that lap pool. Sculpted shoulders and pecs gave way to gently defined abs.

"Are you done?" he asked. "Do I pass muster?" She whipped her eyes to his face. His eyes twinkled with amusement.

Embarrassed, all she could do was nod.

"Then get your ass into this bed, because I have something to prove."

"I'm not sure if this is the best—ahh!" She'd been standing about a foot from the bed, and he hooked one leg around her shins, causing her to topple over onto...the most comfortable bed in the universe. "Oh, my God. This bed is made of clouds or cotton or..." She trailed off, struggling for words to describe the feeling of being utterly enveloped in lightness and comfort.

A rogue thought flittered through her head: This was how he got them. The bed, the insane bathroom. The whole house. *Marcus's girls.*

And now she was one of them.

But before she could let the thought begin to really take hold and demand examination, he settled himself at her feet, grabbed one of them, and started kneading the sole.

"Oh my God," she moaned. It was like the bed in foot-rub form. The feeling of surrendering a burden. The cessation of effort.

She couldn't make herself open her eyes, or even lift her head, which had lolled back against the headboard. "Marcus, you are so *considerate* sometimes."

"No," he said. "It's not consideration; it's ego. It's imperative that I demonstrate that I'm not usually so...hasty."

She started to protest, to say that if he'd been hasty, she'd been hastier, but he kept talking over her. "After a long, hard day walking around, worried about Salt, I think you deserve...a more considered approach."

She could barely hear what he was saying. But he could

keep talking forever as far as she was concerned, as long as he kept doing those insane things to her feet.

Or…he could trace his way up her ankle with his mouth. That would work too. She sighed into the onslaught of his tongue on her calf. And by the time he'd stretched himself over her and begun simultaneously kneading a breast and kissing her neck, she was practically whimpering.

Marcus's girls. This was how it happened.

Screw it. She was going to surrender. There was no choice, really. She'd sort through the fallout later. Except… there was one niggling little reservation she couldn't shake. There was a reason they shouldn't be doing this, but she couldn't quite put her finger on it. Something beyond the fact that it was a Very Bad Idea. Oh! She sat up, shaking him off her. "What about Nate?"

His brow furrowed. "What about him?"

"He's going to come back soon, isn't he?"

"He has a key."

"That doesn't comfort me. There's no door on your lair." Why was she obsessing about the possibility of Nate knowing what was happening? For all she knew he had come back already, when they'd been doing it against the window.

"He'll just drop off the stuff and leave," Marcus said. "He's discreet."

"I don't know. I don't think I can relax enough to have sex knowing that he might walk into the house at any moment."

"We won't have sex." He didn't move though, just let his hands slide down her chest, slip over her nipples, turning them into hardened nubs, and then move down to grab her hips, pressing them down onto the bed as if he were trying to anchor her against an oncoming storm.

"What do you call this, then?" she protested, even as she knew she was going to surrender.

He let the hands that had been anchoring her hips slide a little farther down her legs. Then, spreading them, he buried his face between them. When his tongue made contact with her center, her hips bucked involuntarily.

The hands shot back to her hips, pressing them down hard.

He lifted his head, gracing her with an evil grin. "Cunnilingus," he said, over-enunciating, managing to make the word sound prim and dirty at the same time. "I call this cunnilingus."

Chapter Twelve

So let me see if I can recap. You're pretending to be engaged to this guy. He gave you his mother's TWO CARAT PINK DIAMOND. You made out at your apartment last week. Then you went out and spent the day together and had fun.

But you're not dating. Not even a little bit.

I dunno, kiddo. As far as I can see, the only thing missing is for you guys to actually do the deed. Make sure he can deliver the goods, so to speak.

Rosie sighed. She was trying, for the thousandth time, to compose an overdue reply to an email from Jo. The problem was her answer would have to shine light on a few…omissions in their recent correspondence. And she wasn't fooling anyone because Jo had made the subject line of the email YOU DIDN'T SAY ANYTHING ABOUT MARCUS IN YOUR LAST PAPER LETTER. SPILL THE BEANS, LADY.

It was true. Last week, after Dave — *after Marcus* — Rosie had penned the obligatory Thursday night letter. She'd told the Hummer story. But she hadn't said a word about Marcus. She wasn't really sure why. It was the first time she had ever censored herself with Jo. Her friend knew about that weird, chatty first kiss, so *not* telling her about the intense post-Dave make-out session had been a deliberate choice.

And not really one she could justify.

And with her continued silence, she'd only compounded the lie because now, of course, there was *a lot* more to tell.

Like about how they nearly got kicked out of Edward's for public indecency.

Or made out in a pile of Christian Louboutins.

Both of which paled in comparison to the way she left a body print on Marcus's window yesterday.

And then there was the sexting.

As if on cue, her phone chimed, signaling an incoming text. Her body — her poor, beleaguered body — had been conditioned to respond to that sound. It leaped to attention, a parody of sexual desire as her nipples tightened and moisture gathered between her legs. Eyeing the phone, she kicked the door of her office closed. She had learned that reading Marcus's filthy texts required privacy.

Who knew Mr. Courtly had such a mouth on him?

Who knew she did?

It had started not five minutes after she'd left his house last night. She had fallen asleep after Marcus's tongue nearly killed her. The force of her orgasm, and the day spent walking around with Salt, had been twin forces of exhaustion. After she woke an hour later, she extricated herself with a promise to be in touch soon with news of a shelter space for Salt. What she had wanted to say was *when can we do this again?* But she was playing it cool. Marcus was not real, she reminded herself as she left. Marcus did not do relationships. So probably that had been a one-time thing.

But then, not five minutes after Nate had dropped her off at her place, a text from him arrived.

When can we do that again?

God knew what had possessed her to play coy. Coy wasn't normally her style.

Do what again?

He didn't answer directly. But what he did say made his point rather adequately.

I'm lying in my bed looking at a Rose-sized smudge on my window, and my dick is hard as a rock.

And it had escalated from there. The problem was that he'd flown to Montreal this morning to meet with some of the Magnifique reps for a final discussion before the big pitch. She'd offered to come over and walk Salt a couple times during the day, but he assured her that Nate would be on dog duty. So she was left scrolling through messages that would make her mother disown her and trying—and failing—to get some work done.

Her phone buzzed again. Right. She'd been so busy

remembering old sexts from Marcus that she forgot she had a new one. She swallowed, her throat suddenly dry, and picked up the phone.

ANSWER MY EMAIL!!!!

She laughed out loud. False alarm. It was only Jo. All right. It was time to come clean.

Okay, I'm sitting down to the computer to do it now. Brace yourself.

Ten minutes later, she hit send, having fully spilled the Marcus beans.

Her phone buzzed. Man, Jo was fast. Honestly, her friend was going to be so on her case that Rosie thought she might prefer the time lag of snail mail.

She fumbled the phone as if it were too hot to touch.

Aren't you working?

Done. Trying to get on an earlier flight—no luck so far. What are you wearing?

She shivered a little thrill-chill and typed:

Yellow jeans and a black sweater.

That's not what I'm talking about, and you know it.

Her face heated. She did know.

Red lace.

Should she add that she'd selected her lingerie this morning with great care? She had no idea if she was going to see him tonight. She'd assumed not, given the Montreal trip, but, as it always did with her, hope sprang eternal.

Not that she was hoping for anything serious. She wasn't going to project more onto this thing with Marcus than was there. But a little more pre-Hanukkah fun wouldn't go amiss. And by "a little more fun," of course, she meant "a few dozen more thundering orgasms."

Who is tomorrow's Mr. Thursday Night?

Huh? It took a moment for her brain to catch up. She'd expected, as with their other text exchanges, things to start with red lace and escalate from there.

Not sure yet.

Which was true, but she regretted it as soon as she hit send. She didn't want him thinking she was prevaricating on his account. Because she was forcing herself to go on her regular Thursday date this week. She couldn't let this…thing with Marcus distract her from her larger mission. So she hurriedly added:

I have two candidates.

Which was true. Trueish. She'd been chatting with two men this week and both seemed interested and interesting. She just needed to firm up specific plans with one of them. She'd been a little…distracted.

One's a sculptor, the other a cop.

Which was also true.

There was no answer for a long time. She was so wound up by the time the return ping came that she jumped about a foot.

Go with the cop.

What did she expect? That he was going to register his objection to her date? She needed to woman up here and keep things in perspective.

Why?

I gotta go—the airline is paging me.

She dropped the phone like a hot potato. What had just happened there? That was it? There wasn't going to be any response to the red lace?

It buzzed again. Okay, she needed to calm down. There he was.

I read your email!!!! You have been holding out on me! Holy shit, girl!!!

Rosie groaned and buried her head in her hand. She needed a break from her phone. She needed to get out of her goddamned head and go do something in the actual world.

"Sorry, Jo," she said, muting the phone and heading out the door of her office. "What are you doing tonight?" she asked Hailey when she'd reached reception. "I'm jonesing for some fun. Let's go out."

"I can't," Hailey said. "I have a gig."

"Oh, that's great," Rosie said, because it was what she

was supposed to say. She listened dutifully as Hailey filled her in on the details. The old mental friend Rolodex was looking a little slim these days—too much time spent dating Internet losers.

"Oh, hang on a sec." Hailey handed Rosie a slip of paper. "You have a phone message from when you were at the ravine project meeting earlier—she called the main line looking for you." She grinned. "That might solve your evening social dilemma."

In the "from" field, Hailey had written "Cassie James—girlfriend of Marcus's friend Jack." In the "message" field, "Girl gang karaoke night. Please come."

Aww, those girls were so nice to include her. But she couldn't do karaoke with Marcus's friends.

Could she?

"Thank you!" Rosie called to the driver as she hopped out of the taxi. She was grinning from ear to ear and buzzing from what had turned out to be a wildly fun evening. Marcus's friends were so much fun—at least the female half of his gang.

She tripped as she missed the curb. Okay, she was maybe also buzzing from one too many margaritas. But how was a person supposed to stand up and sing "Sweet Caroline" with one's fake fiancé's friends' girlfriends without a fair amount of liquid courage sloshing around in one's veins?

She wasn't so out of it, though, that she wasn't aware of her surroundings. No, it took more than three margaritas to disable Rosie's stranger-danger spidey sense. So when a dark figure in her peripheral vision moved toward her, she took a step back — and somehow managed to trip over her own feet for the second time in ten seconds.

"Rose."

Ahh! That voice! It was like there was a secret "on" switch in her body that voice had command over.

"Marcus, hi." She'd been going for sophisticated, but she was slurring a little. She cleared her throat. "What are you doing here?"

"When my plane landed, there was a text from Cassie that you needed a ride home. But you weren't at the bar — I must have missed you — so I came back here."

"I'm so glad you're here!" It was out before she realized that response wasn't helping her case on the whole sophisticated front.

"Let's get you inside," he said, putting his arm all the way around her like she needed help walking.

She was about to protest that she was fine. But there was that muscly arm holding her, and his hard chest, which shouldn't have been as comfy as it was on account of the whole hardness thing. So instead of pulling away, she snuggled in closer. It's possible she might have purred. "Why didn't you text me?"

"I did. I was starting to worry about you."

She dug in her purse for her phone. "Oh. Sorry." Then she read a few of them, in which Marcus detailed what he was planning to do to her when she got home. "Oh, really, *really* sorry. It was too loud in there to hear my phone."

He took her keys from her as she was fumbling them out of her purse.

"Don't let Matt out!" she whispered. Or maybe it wasn't

a whisper so much as a shriek. She'd been trying to whisper so as not to wake her neighbors since it was one in the morning, but somehow her calibration was off.

Marcus opened the door a crack, blocking it with his leg, and reached inside and flipped on the light in the entryway. "Looks to be all clear."

They slipped inside, and he said, "Who's Matt? Does he need to be walked?"

As if on cue, Matt hopped into view. She was about to explain that no, Matt did not need to be walked on account of the fact that he was a rabbit, but she was distracted by the fact that Marcus was pulling her out of her coat.

"Does Matt need food? Water? Attention of any kind?"

"No. But *I* need attention of a certain kind." She laughed at her own joke, but Marcus didn't join her.

He finished hanging up both their coats before he spoke. Dipping his head to meet her eyes—he was getting right in her face, actually—he said, "Go into your bedroom and take your clothes off and get into bed."

Every inch of her skin was tingling with anticipation. She'd been thinking earlier that this was the best night she'd had in a long time, but it was about to get even better. She skipped down the hall to comply, listening to him banging around in her kitchen as she stripped. She entertained a moment of indecision when she got to the red lace undies. Did "take your clothes off" mean underwear, too? Nah, she decided, thinking back to how crazy her skivvies had made him yesterday and hopping under the covers.

He came into the room and stood over her. She stayed lying down. From her vantage point, he looked like a superhero. A corporate superhero in his suit—he hadn't even loosened his tie. She wondered if she could get him to leave the suit on. There was something about the contrast between it and her red underwear that was...getting to her. So she threw off the covers.

"Take these." He opened his palm to reveal two Advil. He was holding a giant glass of water in his other hand, which he handed over after she scrambled up to sit against the headboard and popped the pills.

When she tried to set the water down on her bedside table, he said, "Ah, ah, ah. Finish the whole thing."

"I'm not thirsty." In fact, she was so full of nachos and margaritas, she thought she might float away.

"Finish it." He used the same commanding, slightly put-upon tone as that time she'd been in his office.

She finished the water.

Then he took the glass from her and spun on his heel.

"Hey!" she called, vaguely aware that her indignant tone was also not helping with her Mission: Sophistication. She lowered her voice. "Where are you going?"

He came back with the water glass refilled and set it on her bedside table. "I'll be on the sofa if you need me."

Sophistication be damned. "No way, Marcus." She shook her phone at him. "You need to deliver on what you..." She giggled. "What you threatened."

"You're drunk."

"Only a little."

"I don't do drunk hookups."

"It's not like you just picked me up in a bar! We're..." She waved her hand back and forth between them. They were what? She must be drunker than she thought, because she struggled to find words to finish the thought. Or maybe it wasn't the booze. Maybe the whole concept of "we're pretending to be engaged but we're not dating but we are sleeping together except not now because one of us was stupid enough to get drunk and ignore her phone" just didn't *have* a convenient shorthand. "Anyway, you read my texts all day. You know I'm, uh…into it."

"Your judgment is impaired." His voice was clipped, impatient. "I don't do that."

She sighed in frustration and flopped back on the bed. *Why* hadn't she checked her phone? And why was Marcus so goddamned honorable?

He paused on his way out the door. "Try to finish the water. I know you don't want to now, but it will make tomorrow less awful."

She wanted to cry as she heard him moving around in the living room. Actual physical tears were prickling behind her eyeballs. Hanukkah was two days away, and suddenly this lost opportunity seemed like such an enormous, needless waste.

But then the fact that she was so upset made her…more upset. What was she doing? She couldn't get this worked up over the fact that her fake fiancé was too ethical to have drunk sex with her. Sex that wasn't going to lead anywhere was fine. It was fun. But that was all it could be. The lack of it couldn't leave her feeling so…gutted.

She shook her head. It was probably the booze. She was getting maudlin. The lights flicked off in the living room, immersing the apartment in darkness. God, he was just so *upstanding*. Anyone else would have seen her safely home and just left.

"Marcus?" she called tentatively. "You don't have to

stay. I'm fine."

"I'm staying," he said, in a tone that brooked no opposition.

She sighed. "So chivalrous."

"It's not chivalry. It's self-interest."

Huh? "I know you hate being thought of as considerate, but this is really—"

"I don't do drunk hookups, see." He started talking right over her, which, come to think of it, *wasn't* very considerate. "But I don't have any such policy against hungover hookups. And tomorrow morning I plan to do unspeakable things to you. So just shut up and go to bed."

Rosie let the strangled, frustrated noise that rose up her throat answer for her. Several minutes of silence elapsed while she mentally went back through the day's texts and tried to imagine what "unspeakable things" might mean.

"Marcus?"

"For God's sake, go to *sleep*."

"Come in here and sleep with me—just sleep."

"No way."

"Come on. You don't even have a proper pillow out there. I promise I won't ravish you." In fact, she was suddenly overwhelmingly tired, so it wouldn't be too torturous to make good on her word. Today had definitely been a roller coaster of sensation—pent-up desire from all the sexting, crazy-fun at karaoke. But now, the fight was leaving her, energy seeping out like a leaky balloon, leaving her bones mushy.

She had pretty well resigned herself to the fact that he wasn't going to come when she heard his footsteps crossing the apartment. The bed dipped behind her, and even though he didn't touch her, she was acutely, viscerally aware of his presence. She wanted to touch him so badly. It wasn't a pulsing, urgent need to pounce on him, like before. She was still heavy with exhaustion and the pull of sleep was strong. No, she just wanted to…hug him. Which was ridiculous. She was pretty sure the whole fake-fiancé-turned-hookup situation wasn't supposed to involve cuddling.

But then—maybe it was the vestiges of the alcohol in her system—she got a little weepy. Sometimes a person just wanted to feel arms tightening around her with no expectations, no uncertainty. Was that too much to ask? It felt like she'd been on a million dates in the past year but she so rarely really *connected* with anyone. It was like she was surrounded by people but, at the same time, alone.

Screw it. If it was awkward in the morning, she could just pretend not to remember. She was drunk, right? Drunk enough for it to work as an excuse, anyway.

So she rolled over and snuggled up against his side, laying her head on his chest, which was bare. Again, she thought it must have been a violation of the laws of physics that such a hard chest could feel so comforting.

He stayed very still for a moment, and she held her breath. Then his arms closed around her.

She sighed and went to sleep.

When his phone alarm went off the next morning at five thirty, Marcus wondered for a moment if he was the one with the hangover. Because waking up in a strange bed with a woman in his arms was not something that generally happened if he was in his right mind. Even when he was having a casual thing with a woman, sleepovers were rare.

"Sorry," he said, fumbling for the phone as Rose moaned from where her head was tucked into the crook of his arm. He should have remembered to turn off his phone—they'd only gotten four hours of sleep, which was fine for him, but he had a feeling his usual crack of dawn wake-up call was not going to sit well with Rose this morning.

"Mmmmff," she mumbled, writhing against him in a way that woke him up more effectively than a hundred ear-splitting alarms ever could.

"How do you feel?" he asked, grinning at the picture of her all bedraggled and befuddled, then pushing her hair out of her face so he could really look at her. She hadn't taken off her makeup last night, and she had the mascara smudges this morning to prove it. He'd now seen her with makeup, without makeup, and with morning-after makeup.

Interestingly, they all worked for him.

"I feel remarkably okay," she said, flipping onto her back and stretching her arms up to the ceiling—and writhing some more. She needed to quit with that unless she wanted him to make good on his lewd threat of last night. Luckily, she probably didn't even remember it. "I have a little headache, but nothing a couple more Advil and some caffeine won't solve."

She slid over to the edge of the bed and slithered out from under the duvet. "I'll be right back." She took a few steps but then looked back over her shoulder at him. "Unless you want to shower first?"

"First?" he echoed as his brain scrambled to make sense of her meaning. His dick, however, knew what she meant.

Already at half mast, it sprang to attention at the single syllable. Or maybe it was the sight of her standing there in her red lace underwear, all mussed and raccoon-eyed like she'd already been...

"Unspeakable things," she said, interrupting his train of thought. "You promised to do unspeakable things to me this morning, and I'm not letting you out of here until you do." She bit her bottom lip. "Also, I am going to do unspeakable things to you back." Then she smiled, a slow blossoming that gradually lit her face. "Basically, there will be no speaking for the next little while."

He had to close his eyes. He couldn't keep watching her standing there, all gorgeous brown curves and red lace and messy hair, throwing his own lewd threat back at him with what could only be described as bedroom eyes.

As he'd lain awake last night, long after she'd fallen asleep, he'd thought of all the reasons an affair with Rose wasn't a good idea. He had been telling himself that she knew the terms—he had made those explicitly clear—but it still felt unsavory somehow. He could never give Rose what she needed—what she deserved. He just wasn't wired that way. And he would take a vow of chastity before he would treat a woman the way his father had treated his mother. Any woman, but especially Rose. Best, then, to call it— they'd had some fun, but they should quit while it still *was* fun. "I'm not sure if—"

He stopped abruptly as she reached around to unhook her bra and flung it away as if it were made of fire.

Okay then. So much for principles. So much for honor.

He did what any sane, red-blooded man in his position would—he sprang out of bed and grabbed her.

"Hey! I have to brush my teeth!"

"No you don't."

"I really, really do!" she said, laughing as he turned her in place and pointed her toward the bed.

"You really, really don't." He hugged her from behind and walked with his legs wider than hers, which forced her to move along with him, until they got to the edge of the bed.

"You don't even know, Marcus," she said, shrieking as he spun her and pushed her down on her back on the bed.

"I don't even care, Rose," he parroted, falling on top of her but catching himself with his elbows so he wouldn't crush her. He lowered his head but she turned hers, dodging him. They tussled playfully for a few moments until he straddled her and grabbed her upper arms so she was immobilized. She responded by trying to press her lips into a straight, closed line, but since she simultaneously couldn't help grinning, the effect was rather comical. He went in for the kill, but those lips were not opening.

Well, who needed lips? Instead, he pressed his mouth against the side of her throat, which still carried the vestiges of her perfume. He inhaled deeply, letting the scent of it—and her—permeate his head. "What do you always smell like?" he whispered, dragging his lips down to her collarbone.

"Lavender," she said, breathy and low.

Ah, of course. As soon as she named the scent, he recognized it.

"Do you not like it, because—"

In a flash he was up, plunging his tongue into her mouth.

The sound of protest she made quickly gave way to a series of short mewling sounds, and each one ratcheted the tension in him up a little higher, tightening every muscle in his body. Feeling confident that he'd won the "no kissing" battle, he let go of her arms, rolled over onto his side, and dragged his hands up her belly, relishing its soft smoothness. He lightened his touch as he moved upward, wanting to tease her a little, and just barely brushed the skin of her breasts on his way to lightly flicking both nipples.

She inhaled sharply against his mouth and arched her back, seeking firmer pressure.

He did not comply, pulling his hands away entirely and smiling against her lips as he let one hand drift down to tangle in the dark curls where her thighs met. Using the lightest touch he could manage, he brushed one finger against her folds, only to find them warm and wet.

That just about finished him then and there. "Rose," he groaned.

"Shh," she said sharply, sounding like an impossibly sexy librarian and clamping her palm over his mouth. "Unspeakable, remember? No talking."

And then damn if she didn't shove his hand away, sit up, and push him onto his back. Throbbing with want, he let her peel off his boxers and watched her lose her panties, pitching them across the room in the opposite direction from the bra.

She straddled him, but too low, letting her bottom sit on the tops of his thighs. He tried to shuffle himself down the bed to better line them up, but she clamped her own thighs hard around his, held up a censuring finger, and tilted her head, as if scolding a disobedient child.

When he sighed in defeat and let his muscles relax, she trailed one finger down his chest, mimicking the featherlight touch he had just been using with her. Ah, she was giving him a taste of his own medicine, the minx. And it was working, assuming the goal was to drive him mad. He reached up and planted his hands on her hips, intending to move her up so he could press himself against her, but she slapped his hands away.

"Uhhhnnn," he groaned in frustration. Then he eyed her. No speaking, fine—for some reason he was going along with this absurdly erotic game—but were frustrated groans allowed? Apparently so, because she just winked at him and resumed her light exploration of his body, letting her hand come close to but not touch his painfully erect penis. Then she slid her hand around to cup his balls, and for a moment he wished the bed would just burst into flames and immolate him now because that was what was going to happen eventually anyway if he didn't get inside her.

He lifted his head and scowled at her, hoping to telegraph his impatience. It only made her laugh. So he ground his teeth and tried a new tactic to move things along, going straight for her clit with one hand. She reared back, but he'd placed his other hand on her hip, and he clamped down, immobilizing her.

She squirmed, trying to get away from him. But she wasn't trying very hard, and after a few seconds, she went limp and let her head fall back and started rocking her hips in rhythm with his massaging. But she abandoned that rather quickly, seizing control of the game again and wrenching herself away from him, kneeling up with her thighs straightened. He was trying to decide whether to break the stupid no talking rule and demand that she come back down so they could finish what they'd started—or to just *make* her do it—when she suddenly reached over him, yanked open the bedside drawer, procured a condom, rolled it over him, and plunged down on the length of him.

A sound ripped from his throat that was half her name, half strangled cry. But she didn't seem to mind that he'd spoken. She didn't even seem to notice—her eyes were closed and she leaned back, her arms behind her bracing herself on his thighs as she rode him. He put his hand back on her clit and let the incredible sensation of her tightness wash over him as she bucked wildly. He was trying to hold on, to hold back the tidal wave, when she suddenly lifted her head, opened her eyes, and locked her gaze on his. Most women closed their eyes as they came—but leave it to Rose to do things her own way. He watched the orgasm wash over her while she watched him. A big, openmouthed smile blossomed as it started, and she heaved a great breath in and held it. God, it was almost like she was channeling something otherworldly, radically opening herself to experience. She was all in—leaving nothing of herself apart from what was happening to her body. It was a ridiculous thing to think, but for a moment he had the notion that he was lucky to be able to witness this total abandonment.

When she broke her own no speaking rule and gasped his name as she started pulsing and tightening around him, he abandoned his analysis of the situation and surrendered, grabbing her hips and thrusting hard, keeping his gaze on hers as pleasure exploded up his spine.

Rosie had a lot of problems. But right now the primary one seemed to be that she no longer had any bones in her body. And, hey, if she never got out of bed again, probably a lot of her other problems would disappear on their own. Taking a deep breath to try to slow her undignified panting, she stared at the ceiling.

What should she say? What *did* one say after the most epic, bone-shattering sex in the history of humankind? She wished she could think of something clever, something to break the ice—the metaphorical ice because they had turned the bedroom into an inferno—and smooth the way for…whatever was going to come next.

"Why do you have the word *action* stenciled on the wall above your bed?"

She burst out laughing and turned to face Marcus, finding him lying on his side, propping his head up with one hand, and looking adorably bewildered.

"Oh my God! I need to either finish that or get rid of it."

"Finish it? Were you going to add *lights, camera*?" He swiveled his head around, theatrically looking around the room. "Are you filming this?"

She swatted his chest—oh, that chest!—and said, "My best friend Jo—you know, the one I write to?" He nodded. "She was here two summers ago, and she was pregnant. She'd gone a little bananas at home getting the nursery set up. She'd stenciled some nursery rhyme crap on the wall of her baby's room at home."

"Ah!" He grinned as he started gathering his clothes. "Nursery rhyme crap. A well-known genre."

"Yeah, well, she was on fire with the stenciling and decided to stencil something here. I was dead set against it. Meanwhile, the Mr. Thursday Night project was in crisis. Remember the guy I told you about who ended up being married?"

"I do."

She wanted to tell him to stop pulling on his jeans, but that wasn't rational. "Well, I had just found out." She paused, wondering how much more to say. "It was a little heart-breaking, actually, because otherwise, he had seemed so... great." It still hurt to think back to that night she found out there was a Mrs. Asshole to go along with the Mr. she'd been hanging out with—and sleeping with. Jo had arrived just as she was moving from the weepy betrayed stage to the righteous angry stage. "He was very smooth, this guy. He said all the right things."

"And what did he say to his wife when he was with you?"

She shrugged. "I don't know. He was a good talker. He only got busted because she found some texts he'd sent me, and she contacted me and we put two and two together." He whistled in disbelief. She didn't want his reaction to turn into pity, so she plowed on with the story. "Anyway, I decided I was done with smooth talkers and vowed to judge people solely by their actions from then on. I told Jo that my new motto was 'Actions speak louder than words.' I may have threatened to get it tattooed on my forehead."

He snorted. "So she decided to stencil it above your bed?"

"Yes. To remind me. One day while I was at work. I came home to find my pregnant best friend on a rickety step stool painting in a poorly ventilated room, so I shut that shit down by solemnly swearing to finish the job after she left."

"And it's been what? A year and a half?"

"It's ridiculous, of course. But I haven't quite been able to make myself paint over it," Rosie said, eyeing Marcus's ass, which managed to look amazing even in his suit pants, as he bent to put his socks on.

"Rose Verma, they broke the mold when they made you."

She'd been about to ask him if he wanted to shower, hoping he would interpret it as an offer to shower *with her*, when he said, "So, did you go with the sculptor or the cop for tonight?"

The question might as well have been a bucket of ice water poured over her head. She had completely forgotten about her usual Thursday night activities. Rosie blinked. "Um, the sculptor," she said, almost choking on the answer. But really, the question was fine. Welcome, in fact. Because she needed to return to the mindset she'd been in yesterday, even as they were flirting via text. This thing with Marcus had started as a little quid pro quo—a website and a big donation in return for a little playacting. And if it had now become something else—something fun, *something scorching*—it was important to remember that it was necessarily limited. It wasn't like either of them could just be with the other, given their opposing outlooks on love and life. So the Mr. Thursday Night project was just as important as it had always been. More so, in fact, given that she was almost out of time.

"What the hell?" Marcus teased, making a funny face at her in the mirror he was looking in to tie his tie. "I told you to pick the cop."

Oh, but he was gorgeous. It almost hurt to look at him, standing there getting dressed in front of her full-length mirror. As if he did this all the time. As if he did this all the time *here*.

She swallowed the lump in her throat. "I know. You're

probably right. But how often do you meet a sculptor? That's like the opposite job from a management consultant."

He turned. "Nate is picking me up in ten minutes. You want a ride to work?"

She shook her head. "You think my style you're always admiring can be produced in ten minutes?" She was going for humor, because humor was safe. Humor would ease the way as they parted this morning.

But he didn't laugh. Just looked at her, assessing. "Rose, you've got style standing there naked as the day you were born."

She opened her mouth, found she didn't know how to respond, and then closed it and grabbed a robe.

"Good luck with the sculptor," he said, and then he was gone.

Chapter Thirteen

Marcus was faced with a dilemma. He couldn't go to Rose's apartment because there was no dog there he could pretend needed his care, and he wasn't quite desperate enough to offer to babysit a rabbit.

In fact, he had his own canine interloper to worry about, and she was, in fact, lying on top of him as he lay on his bed, running through the Magnifique pitch in his head. As if she knew he was thinking about her, Salt snorted and cuddled in closer.

He also couldn't just tell Rose to come to his place. That was something a boyfriend would do. And he was not Rose's boyfriend. He was no one's boyfriend. In fact, Rose was out with someone else tonight, someone who might become her boyfriend. And if not that guy, eventually one of the Mr. Thursday Nights was going to stick.

He needed to remember where the line was with them. The soul-shattering sex they'd had that morning couldn't change things. Marcus was a man of discipline. Discipline was how he had built the agency from nothing. Discipline had allowed him to walk away from his father's money.

And discipline was what was going to keep him from ruining Rose's chance at a real relationship. Discipline was going to keep him from becoming his father. So far, he'd succeeded, except for the part where he'd never not grown bored by any particular woman after a few weeks. He had to accept that he had inherited his father's cold heart. But what he chose to do about it was up to him. And he wasn't doing that to Rose. She deserved better than his mother had gotten from his father. They just had to get through Hanukkah, which, ironically, was now more important to her than to him, and then everything could go back to normal.

The doorbell rang, so he sat up, gently dumping a whining Salt on the floor and heading for the stairs.

Discipline, he said to himself as he jogged down to the first floor. He was *not* going to Rose's apartment after he'd dispatched whoever was at the door.

Maybe he'd take a swim this evening, even though he'd already done thirty laps when he got home from work.

Discipline.

He swung open the door.

"Hi."

What was the opposite of discipline? Surrender?

Because when Rose shot him a wicked smile and said, "I should have texted, but I just decided to come," discipline went out the fucking window.

He looked at his watch. Ten thirty. Not terribly late, but she obviously hadn't bailed on her date like last week. He stepped aside and gestured her in. "What happened to the sculptor?"

She sighed and shrugged out of her coat to reveal a swingy orange dress that fit her so well it made his teeth hurt. "I hardly know where to start." She kicked off the lemon yellow heels she'd gotten at Leona's party. "Well, that's not true. I do know where to start. He sculpted my boobs."

"*What?*" Had she posed for him? What the hell?

Down, boy. Not his business. *Discipline.*

"We went to dinner first. On paper, it was a good match. He was a vegetarian, too. We went to a fondue place and had cheese fondue."

"Because this date happened in 1979?" he couldn't resist saying.

She ignored him, just moved into his living room. He thought she might plop down on the sofa, but she kept going, heading for the kitchen at the back of the house. He followed.

"He was very...granola. But in some ways, so am I, right?"

She didn't seem to be waiting for an answer, just sat on one of the stools at the kitchen island. "Do you have any wine? The sculptor only drank biodynamic wine, and the fondue place didn't have any."

Grinning, he opened the door to the under-counter wine rack and said, "What's your pleasure?"

"My pleasure is wine."

He selected and uncorked a bottle of 1985 cabernet sauvignon as she talked, relishing the fact that she would not be impressed if he told her the current market value of the bottle was five hundred bucks.

"He asked me to go back to his place. He wanted to show me his work. So I thought, okay, why not? I'm not really feeling it, but I've been starting to think I've been judging guys too quickly. Maybe it's too much to ask that you're going to have instant chemistry with someone."

He set her wine in front of her, resisting pointing out that when their hands brushed as she took it, the air around them practically crackled.

She lifted the glass and chugged about forty bucks worth of wine in under three seconds. "So I get there, and what he wants to show me is *my boobs*."

He shook his head, not understanding.

"Marcus." His name in her low, pleading tone reminded him of something else. Reminded his *cock* of something else. "He sculpted his vision of what my boobs would look like based on his impression of me from photos and from our email exchanges."

He choked back a laugh and watched her down another forty bucks. "And was he close?"

She scrunched up her nose. "He was actually spot on. But that is not the point! There was also something else."

"What?" His mind began to race, imagining this creepy Play-Doh dude doing something truly sinister.

"His name is Axel. But it turns out he spells it all low-ercase—first and last. I thought he was just lazy when he was texting—you know how some people don't bother with capital letters?—but no, he actually spells his name all low-ercase." She threw back the last bit of her cabernet. "People who spell their names all lowercase always say it's because they're protesting something. It's supposed to be a statement against the oppressive establishment or something. But all it does is call attention to them and their enormous egos."

"And that's just not attractive?" he asked. He could see

how a woman who spent her life actively working to save the environment and who prized action above talk so much she had painted it on her wall would be unimpressed with small-a axel.

She thunked her glass down like she'd just thrown back a shot. "Exactly."

"Let's go swimming." It was out before he could think better of it.

"I don't have a suit."

He just raised his eyebrows, waiting for her to get it. Watching the smile blossom as she did caused his cock to jerk to attention. And then she was up, walking toward the door to the basement, unzipping her dress as she went.

She paused at the edge of the pool to unhook her bra—some kind of pink satin thing. "But we also need to talk about Hanukkah at some point. For real. Like, are you picking us up? What are we going to say to my mom to really convince her? That's why I came. We can't just keep having sex and not talking."

He tried not to laugh. Having sex and not talking sounded pretty much perfect to him. But she had a point. He had no idea how astute her mother was, how hard they were going to have to work to pull one over on her. And unlike his father, Rose's mother mattered.

"Got it," he said, intending to shed his clothes to match her state of undress. "But later." It was hard to get undressed, though, when he couldn't tear his eyes from the sight of her nipples pebbled from the cold—and maybe, he flattered himself, from desire. He loved looking at her—all of her. She was such an intriguing mix of qualities that should be contradictory. She'd told him about being bullied as a kid, and part of her did seem to be trying desperately to fit in—to find a boyfriend and settle down. But she had self-confidence in spades. She always seemed completely comfortable in her skin, and took joy in leveraging her unusual beauty to its best advantage.

She put her hands on her hips, which only functioned to call attention to the way they curved. "If you're just going to stand there staring, can you at least take your clothes off so I can stare back?"

"I don't know," he teased. "I'm actually really enjoying just looking at you. I was thinking maybe I'd just stay here on the edge and watch you swim."

"Yeah?" she said, her tone a challenge as she walked toward him. "I don't think I approve of your plan."

"So what are you going to do about it?" he taunted, making a "bring it" gesture and thinking maybe she'd come over and help him get undressed.

She did come over, but she didn't help with his clothes.

She pushed him in.

He hit the water laughing, so water flooded into his open mouth, and he came up coughing.

"Oh my gosh!" she said, diving in. "I'm sorry! Are you okay?"

Facing away from her, he kept coughing until he could feel her proximity. Then he turned around and splashed her.

"Ah! You bastard!"

A water fight to end all water flights ensued. But after a few minutes, the tussling and splashing gave way to tussling and kissing, which in turn gave way to just kissing. Somehow, without him noticing, she had wrapped her legs around his still jeans-clad waist. Writhing against him, she arched her back and shoved a breast toward him. He was only too happy to oblige, licking his way up the soft flesh and taking the nipple that had been tormenting him earlier into his mouth. She whimpered, and suddenly it seemed criminal that he was still wearing his clothes. He took a primal satisfaction at the wail she emitted when he pulled away. "I just have to get these clothes off," he said, hoisting himself up to sit on the side.

The minute he'd shucked off his jeans, her mouth was on him.

"Rose," he growled, disconcerted, one part of him tempted to push her away, because he had intended to get right back to her breasts, the other part...not so much.

The other part won. How could it not when he was looking down at a drenched, naked Rose Verma with her lips wrapped around his cock? He had to close his eyes against the sight, in fact, because otherwise he was going to come immediately, and he wanted to enjoy the ride for a while. He thought about the first time he had seen her, sitting primly in her floral wallpapered office, then rolling toward him on her office chair, the perfect train wreck of a woman to irritate his father. Could he ever have imagined this? Probably not, given that he dropped her off that evening at her date with another man.

But then, she'd come to him tonight from a date with another man.

He shoved the thought aside as her mouth slid up and down, gaining speed. Tension gathered in his balls and lower back. He groaned from the pure gut-wrenching pleasure of it. She opened her eyes at the sound and looked up at him—and smiled. Not with her mouth, obviously, which was otherwise engaged, but with her eyes.

"Oh, fuck!" he groaned as he came.

"Okay, so let's talk about Hanukkah."

"Oh, right." Rosie had forgotten about that. She sighed. There was nothing like a toe-curling orgasm to take a girl's mind off her upcoming cross-cultural, fake-engaged Hanukkah party. The water up here was so warm—after he'd had his orgasm in the cold water of the lap pool, they'd moved to his giant soaker tub for hers. She was now so satiated and sleepy that even lifting her head from his chest as they lay—her back to his front—in the water seemed difficult. Plotting to deceive her mother over latkes felt like the equivalent of solving cold fusion. "Also, I've been forgetting to tell you that the shelter called today. They can take Salt."

"Great. Leave me the info, and I'll have Nate drop her off tomorrow."

Another sigh. "So, Hanukkah." Could she just hold her breath and go under the water until it was all over?

"I think the best thing to do is to keep it simple," he said, lightly trailing his hand back and forth from her knee, which poked out of the water, to her hipbone, which was submerged. "We met at a Habitat event—that's totally plausible. That's what my family already assumes."

She yawned. "And then what happened?"

"We don't even need to make stuff up. We started spending time together. I took care of your dogs, we went on bike rides. We don't have to really lie about anything except…" He shifted beneath her, as if he were suddenly uncomfortable.

"Except the part where we're in love," she finished, trying to keep the bitterness out of her tone.

He cleared his throat. "Right."

"I'm just afraid my mother is going to know something isn't right. It's already super weird that I never told her about someone I'm supposedly planning on marrying."

"Well…" Marcus's hand stayed underwater and slowly began drifting toward her inner thigh. "You may have noticed that there's a certain amount of…chemistry between us."

Rosie gasped as his hand found its target. There was no way she could come again so soon.

"We can use that to our advantage," he said, starting to draw slow, lazy circles around her clit.

"And what?" She struggled to keep her voice under control, even as her hips seemed to be arching, of their own accord, into his touch. "We'll jump each other after the lighting of the menorah?"

He chuckled in her ear. "No. My point is just that some minor PDA might go a long way toward helping our cause. It's certainly better than more talking."

"Yeah, talking is overrated," she whispered.

"When this is done, some of my best memories of you are going to be the non-talking ones," he said.

When this is done. It was like someone had turned on the cold tap and flooded the tub. Which was stupid because it wasn't like she didn't know what was going to happen after Hanukkah was over—after their stupid engagement game was over. She was going to give the shiny ring back and take her shiny new website, and that would be that.

So why did it feel like she was about to burst into tears?

She shifted, turning, taking herself out of range of his touch. "I should go home."

"Really?" He was trying to catch her eye, and she was trying not to let it be caught. But then, deciding that just made her look pathetic and desperate, she lifted her gaze, looked directly into those gorgeous, wise blue-gray eyes.

It hit her all at once.

She was in love with Marcus.

I'm in love with Marcus.

Rosie texted Jo from the cab. To her immense relief, the return text arrived almost immediately.

Of course you are.

The phone rang. Rosie, who had managed so far to hold back the sobs that had been threatening since her awkward middle-of-the-night exit from Marcus's house, panicked.

The ringing stopped.

Pick up the phone, Rosie.

Then it started again.

Her hand shook as she lifted the phone to her ear. "What are you doing? Nobody's dead. We don't do the phone."

"I'm changing things up," said Jo. "That's what you do when things aren't working—you change."

Hearing the voice of someone who loved her made the tears come. It was like when she was a kid and she'd manage to hold it together at school, to be defiant even, and then she'd get home and take one look at her mother and start wailing.

"Everything okay, miss?" said the driver, glancing at her in the rearview mirror.

"Rosie, I'm going to say something you're not going to like," Jo said.

She nodded at the driver and sniffed. "Okay, hit me."

"Did you ever think that all your failed Thursday night dates have one thing in common, and that thing is you?"

It was like a punch to the gut, her best friend turning on her. Jo might as well have announced she was joining the Ashley and Tiffany clique.

"Have you been listening to anything I've been saying the past few years?" *No, because you're too busy with your perfect husband and your perfect baby.* She hated herself for being jealous, but she couldn't help it.

"I have. But I've also been listening to what you haven't been saying."

"Which is what?" Rosie didn't even bother trying to stop the sneer in her voice. This was just rich. She'd been hoping for sympathy, but apparently she was going to get armchair pop psychology bullshit instead.

"You never give anyone a chance." When Rosie started to protest, Jo raised her voice. "Let me finish. You've had a lot of objectively bad dates, yes. But what about that teacher?"

"He barfed all over me!"

"Yes, but you had fun before that. And he emailed you several times abjectly apologizing. People make mistakes, Rosie. He was probably just nervous because he *liked* you. And you blew him off."

Rosie blinked rapidly, trying to absorb all this impossible

information, as the cab pulled up at her building. She threw some money at the driver and got out.

"And what about Hummer Dave?" said Jo, her speech gathering speed. "You didn't even give him *one* chance. And all those animals you foster? What the hell? It's like you don't *want* anything or anyone to stick. You sabotage yourself by setting these impossibly high standards that no one can meet. You're afraid to let people get too close."

Staggering toward the front door of her building, her lungs feeling like they were going to explode, Rosie had to reach out and steady herself against the brick facade.

"And you do it to me, too," said Jo. "This thing where we're only allowed to text and email?"

"But that's our thing," Rosie protested weakly.

"No," said Jo. "That's *your* thing. Do you know how hard it is to type and breastfeed?" Jo's voice caught. Rosie had made her best friend cry. "And do you know how many hours of the day I spend breastfeeding, bored out of my skull, wishing for nothing more than a little adult conversation? But you have these rules, these ideas about how our relationship is supposed to be. The letter thing was cute when we were kids. But…"

Rosie was slammed for the second time that evening with a horrible truth. She *did* push people away. The thought that she was doing it to Jo, too, nearly broke her heart.

"Anyway," Jo whispered. "Of course you're in love with Marcus."

Her whirling mind struggled to make the connection between her feelings for Marcus and what Jo had just said. "I'm not sure I follow."

"You weren't sabotaging yourself with Marcus because

you weren't *trying* with him."

Oh, God. "Because I thought he was off-limits. Because he *is* off-limits. A self-professed womanizer not looking to settle down. A millionaire totally out of my league. I didn't have to hold him at arm's length because that was his permanent location from the start."

"Ding, ding, ding," said Jo, laughing and crying at the same time.

"Jo," Rosie whispered, "I'm so sorry."

"Yeah, yeah, you can apologize later. Maybe on one of our upcoming Thursday night *phone calls.* The question is, what are you going to do about Marcus?"

"What can I do? He doesn't do relationships. He's told me that about a thousand times."

"Yeah, so? I'll say it again. What are you going to do about it?"

"What? Ask him to change the rules for me? I think he's somehow afraid he's going to become like his father. I can't compete with that shit."

There was just silence on Jo's end.

"He doesn't *do* relationships," Rosie protested.

"If you want something good, Rosie, you have to take a risk. That's just the way the world is."

"But—"

Jo, shutting down Rosie's protest said, "Happy Hanukkah."

Then she hung up.

Chapter Fourteen

As he headed to Rose's the next afternoon, Marcus sent a silent prayer to whomever might be listening up there that they could pull this off—for Rose's sake. Sure, fooling his father, which had been the initial point of the game, would be satisfying. But not ruining Rose's relationship with her mother? That was something worth lighting a Hanukkah candle for.

Twenty-four hours ago, he would have said they had it in the bag. But something weird had happened last night in the tub. His fearless, confident Rose had…disappeared. That was the only way he could think to describe it. One minute she'd been writhing under his hand, losing herself in sensation, as she did so easily—his dick stirred just thinking about it—and the next, she couldn't get away from him fast enough.

As he rounded the corner and her building came into view, he could see her waiting on the curb with an older woman next to her, the falling snow accumulating on their coats. She didn't recognize his car because he was driving himself. He took a moment to study her unobserved. She was wearing the "non-crazy" coat, and her hair was piled on top of her head in some sort of updo. His heart gave a little twist to see her standing there with her mother, who, though she was shorter and her hair was streaked with silver, looked remarkably like her daughter.

He shuddered to think of Rose telling her mom, a few weeks from now, that they had broken up. God, he was a total dick, dragging not one, but two, innocent women into the pit of vipers that was his family.

But now that Rose's mom was involved, they *had* to pull this off. Failure was not an option.

He hopped out of the car. "Rose, Mrs. Verma. You should have waited inside. I would have come up."

Rose's face lit up—did he dare hope that she was back? That whatever had happened last night had been an aberration? A case of pre-Hanukkah nerves, maybe?

But then, just as quickly, it shuttered. "Nice wheels, Marcus." The smile that accompanied the jibe didn't reach her eyes.

He suddenly thought maybe he *should* have had Nate drive. The Porsche's backseat was tiny. And did it come off as obnoxious and ostentatious?

More importantly, why did he care? They just had to play their roles and get through the night. And he was a CEO with a Porsche. Nothing wrong with that, and no role-playing required on that front.

He handed an unsmiling Mrs. Verma a wrist corsage. "A token for the guest of honor. It's a pleasure to finally meet you. I'd been intending to ask your permission to ask Rose to marry me." He smiled at Rose. "But I'm afraid we got a little bit ahead of ourselves."

Rose insisted on taking the backseat, and he kept glancing at her in the rearview mirror. She never met his eyes.

After a minute of silence, Mrs. Verma said, "When is the wedding?"

He looked over and confirmed that she was talking to him, not Rose. "Uh, we haven't decided yet, but really, whenever Rose wants it to be."

"Rose is being noncommittal, which is why I'm asking you."

When he didn't answer right away, she lobbed another question at him. "Can you afford this car?"

His eyes went to Rose, and this time she *was* looking back at him—and trying not to laugh. Well, that was an improvement.

"I can. I bought it with cash."

Mrs. Verma nodded. "I like it."

"I'll drive you home in it tonight."

"You can't drive her all the way to Aurora," Rose protested.

"Why not? I don't want my future mother-in-law on a late train when I can just as easily drive." He meant it, even if the future-mother-in-law part was a lie. There was no need for Rose's mother to schlep back downtown to the train station.

Mrs. Verma smiled. "I like your car. You, I'm not sure about yet."

"Mother!" exclaimed Rose from the backseat.

He laughed—genuinely. He could see where Rose got that unshakable streak of confidence. "Well, I'm sure about you, Mrs. Verma," he said, surprised that it was the truth, "so I'll just have to wait you out."

Rosie was just beginning to think they might actually pull this off. The car ride over had been...surprisingly not fraught. Marcus had played her mother pitch perfectly, being deferential but not trying too hard.

At the house, Marcus's aunt Rachel greeted them, if not warmly, at least without any overt show of disdain. Her mother was introduced to the family, and was urged to visit the buffet, which was laden with a truly astonishing amount of food.

"Hanukkah is really only a minor holiday," said Ruth, taking her mother's arm.

"It gets trumped up because of Christmas," Marcus added, taking her other arm. "We'll light the menorah later and spin the old dreidel, but really, for us, it's all about the food. But do you know the story? I'll fill you in while we hit the buffet."

Rosie watched Marcus help her mother fill a plate, and it felt like she'd been punched in the gut. Everything Jo had said was right. She loved Marcus Rosemann. *She loved Marcus Rosemann.* How weird was that?

The other stuff was true, too, about her being afraid to let anyone—human or animal—get too close. But, in a warped sort of way, she was glad about that because if she'd had all her psychological ducks in a row earlier, she never would have met Marcus. And even if tonight was the end, she wouldn't trade her time with him for anything.

There was one more thing Jo had been right about: She had to tell him. She had to utter those three scary words. It was going to make things awful and awkward, but what did that really matter? If things were over anyway, what was a little awkwardness in exchange for speaking her truth?

And it wasn't just about her. She wanted Marcus to know that he was kind and funny, despite his sometimes-brusque exterior. She wanted him to know that she admired him for making his own way in the world, for earning the success he'd enjoyed. She wanted him to know that when he smiled at her with a day's worth of beard growth, her heart flopped around like a fish out of water.

She wanted him to know that she loved him. That, even if he didn't feel the same way, he was worthy of love.

Because she didn't think anyone had ever told him that, except maybe his mother.

Rosie was terrified, but she kept repeating Jo's words inside her head: *If you want something good, you have to take a risk.*

She was going to do it tonight. Even if she had to corner him, blurt it out, then flee with her mother in tow, Porsche ride home be damned. She glanced at her mom, who was being led to a cushy-looking upholstered chair and set up with a portable tray to rest her plate on.

She sighed. Damn it, maybe not tonight. Because she had to remember what the priority was here. God help her, it was bamboozling her poor mother. And fleeing wasn't conducive to bamboozlement.

She didn't have too much time to think about it, though, because a couple of cousins waved her over and launched into a friendly interrogation. And then Marcus was back, presenting her with a plate laden with latkes, salad, and kugel, nary a dead animal in sight. Hand resting on her lower back—resting a little lower than her lower back, actually, which sent a little shiver of electricity through her—he led her to sit next to her mom.

Everyone was laughing and chatting in little clusters around an enormous living room, balancing plates on their laps. The whole thing was less formal—and less stressful—than she had anticipated.

Until Marcus's father arrived, appearing in the room seemingly from out of nowhere.

A hush fell over the crowd. God, it was like that Voldemort dude from *Harry Potter* had arrived. He wasn't related to these people. Why didn't they just rise as one and, like, expel him?

Mr. Rosemann's eyes scanned the room, and when they landed on Rosie, they lingered for a moment before he transferred his attention to her mother. Rosie had the odd impulse to throw her body in front of her mom to protect her. Marcus's arm suddenly appeared around her shoulder. It had an immediate distracting effect. Man, he was good at this. She snuggled in. Even though they were only acting, he felt too good not to.

"It's time to light the menorah now that you're here, Bart," said Rachel, dimming the lights. It sat on a low table in the center of the room. Everyone grew quiet and put their forks down.

A young cousin lit the center candle, then used that to light a single candle on one end of the menorah. Rachel began reciting a prayer in Hebrew, and Marcus translated for her and her mother, whispering: "Blessed are you, O Lord our God, ruler of the universe, who has sanctified us with your commandments and commanded us to light the candles of Hanukkah."

Rose turned from the proceedings to look at Marcus. His face was bathed in candlelight, and he was so impossibly dear to her. A lump rose in her throat. There was something magical happening here, even if none of them other than Rachel were observant. People had been doing this—lighting the candles, telling the story of the Maccabees—for centuries. It was bigger than all of them. She wanted so badly to be part of this, to belong here as Marcus's real girlfriend, even if his family would always see the unsuitable girl from the wrong side of the tracks.

"Marcus, I—" She choked on the words.

"What's wrong?" Concern unfurled across his beautiful face as his brow furrowed. A hand came up to her face, resting on the side of her cheek.

"Stop pawing your girlfriend, Marcus, and pay attention," said Mr. Rosemann.

"Bart," said Rachel. "It's all right. We're done."

"She's not my girlfriend. She's my fiancée." Marcus took her hand and squeezed, the tension radiating off him in waves.

"We haven't met," said her mother, standing and moving toward Marcus's father. The whole room watched her mother cross the room and offer a hand to the scowling patriarch. "I'm Sonya Verma."

He didn't take it. He just stood there, looking at her blankly, like she was speaking another language.

"Bart," said Ruth in a stage whisper.

Rosie hadn't been prepared for this. She'd expected passive aggression, small slights. Not an outright snubbing.

The doorbell rang, and it had the effect of draining some of the tension from the proceedings. Cary, who had been standing nearest the door, answered it.

It was Lauren. Rosie didn't know she'd been invited, but it was nice to see a friendly face. Or what would have been a friendly face had she not looked like she had the weight of the world on her shoulders.

"Marcus," she said from the entryway. "I need to talk to you. Your phone is off. I'm sorry to interrupt, but it's urgent."

"What is it?" said Marcus, still staring at his father. Rose thought it would have to be something pretty earth-shattering to prompt him to stand down from his father.

"I'm not sure everyone needs to hear what—"

"Just tell me." He spoke to Lauren but he kept his eyes on his father.

Lauren waited a beat before saying, "Gail stole the Magnifique pitch," in a calm, even tone that belied the bombshell she was dropping. "Jody has been working for her all along. I just caught her photographing the final presentation."

"Gail Abram?" said Cary.

"Gail wouldn't do that," Marcus's father scoffed. "The Abrams are old family friends."

That was it. Rosie was done taking shit from this bully. She whipped her head around. "Just like she wouldn't sell photos of us to a gossip site?"

"Photos of you two cooking up a scheme to deceive us all with this fake engagement bullshit, you mean," said Mr. Rosemann, voice dripping with scorn.

What the hell?

"Thought you had us all fooled, did you, Miss Verma?" Mr. Rosemann said. "The rest of them maybe." He gestured toward the assembled family. "But not me." He curled his lip and turned his attention to Marcus. "Gail overheard you plotting to pretend to be engaged, and she took the pictures.

The day after the ball, she came to me with the news—and the photos. Because she cares about this family, whether you choose to believe it or not, Marcus."

"She came to you with the photos? So how did they end up on *Gossip TO*, then?" Cary asked.

"Bart," Ruth said, her tone full of censure. "You didn't."

"Of course I didn't." He sniffed as if the thought of interacting with a rag like *Gossip TO* was beneath him. "I merely instructed Gail to do something with them that would embarrass you, Marcus. Give you a taste of your own medicine—turnabout for all these years you've embarrassed me."

Because a photo of Marcus with Rose would be inherently embarrassing. *Enough to get him to cave and come back to the family firm? To marry someone who was the opposite of her?* Rose ordered herself not to cry from the humiliation.

Mr. Rosemann looked at Marcus. "You were trying to manipulate me, and I won't stand for it."

"I learned from the best," said Marcus quietly, his face devoid of emotion, which was scarier than shouting would have been. He stood up. "I have to go." He looked at Rosie. "I'm sorry." To Lauren he said, "I owe you an apology, too. This wouldn't have happened if I hadn't been..." He glanced back at Rosie, and he didn't even need to finish the sentence for it to be a knife to her heart. "If I hadn't been so distracted by my stupid prank." He cleared his throat. "I'll meet you at the office. We'll start over." Lauren nodded and slipped out the door.

He was just going to *leave*? "No!" Rosie cried, beyond caring that she was making this train wreck of a situation worse. Marcus's father had humiliated her. Marcus had called what they had a "stupid prank." But she kept thinking about what Jo said. About telling the truth, taking a risk. The tears started before she even spoke. "I love you," she whispered.

Gasps echoed all around the room.

"Don't go," she added. "Not like this."

"Game's over, Rose," he said. "We lost. You were a great sport."

A great sport? It really *had* been just a game to him, hadn't it? More tears slipped from the corners of her eyes, and she swiped angrily at them. But, swallowing hard, and even though she knew she was just making herself more wretched, she managed to get one more sentence out. "I love you for real."

He stared at her for a long moment. Then he shook his head. Of course he did. What had she thought? That her love was enough?

That he would choose *her*?

"I don't love you, Rose. I can't. I'm not capable of it." Then he turned to his father. "And you." The venom in his voice was chilling. "For the record, those pictures didn't embarrass me. This miserable family should be so *lucky* as to have Rose Verma join it. She's worth more than every cent of your goddamned fortune."

His father started to say something, but Marcus held up a hand, radiating power and authority. "You and I are done."

Then Rosie watched Marcus Rosemann walk out of her life forever, without flinching, without looking back. The joke was on her that she was so shocked. After all, he'd warned her about this. He'd gotten what he'd paid for, and so had she. She had her website and her donation. And he had his train wreck of a fake fiancée, a role she had inhabited to perfection. The perfectly imperfect woman.

Chapter Fifteen

When Marcus stepped off the elevator on the forty-ninth floor, he ran into Jack and Dax on their way down. Between the early darkness and the holiday—and having the rug utterly pulled out from under him—he'd forgotten that it was just a regular weekday. It was eight, so the floor was mostly empty, but it was no surprise to see the other two CEOs there.

"I thought it was Hanukkah," Dax said.

"Where's Rose?" Jack asked. "We're meeting Amy and Cassie at Edward's. You guys want to come?"

"Rose and I broke up." He tried to brush past them, but of course he should have known that would be impossible.

Dax said, "Whoa."

"Yeah, and it turns out a rival agency stole our Magnifique pitch. Happy fucking Hanukkah."

"The pitch for tomorrow?" Jack asked, incredulous.

"Yeah, so if you'll excuse me, I've got an all-nighter to

pull. Lauren is waiting."

Lauren *was* waiting. His loyal partner. The only person in this shit world he could trust. They would just have to do what they'd done in the old days—stay up all night and pull a concept out of thin air.

"Hey," she said, flashing him a weary smile when he arrived in her office. "This is all my fault. I'm sorry."

"It's not your fault," he said. "It's mine. I wasn't here. I've been mentally checked out, off my game."

She looked at him for a long moment. "You know what? It's actually Jody's fault."

Why, he suddenly wondered, was Lauren only executive creative director? Why was their company called the Rosemann Agency? Because he'd started it six months before hiring her? What was the matter with him? "You should be partner," he said. "We should be Rosemann-Daelin."

"Whoa," she said. "What the hell is the matter with you?"

"He just got dumped."

He turned to find Dax and Jack in the doorway.

"I assume," Dax added, "that you're the dumpee and not the dumper. I'm giving you credit here for not being a total idiot."

Lauren raised her eyebrows. "Excuse me, what?"

"We're a little busy," Marcus said, not bothering to tamp down his annoyance.

"We brought beer," said Jack, plunking a six-pack down on Lauren's desk.

Dax grinned. "Emergency stash for late night coding binges. We thought you might need it. You *were* the dumpee, though, right? Because otherwise, I don't think you deserve this."

"Oh my God, Marcus," said Lauren, as he buried his head in his hands and bit the insides of his cheeks to keep from screaming. "Just tell them."

Still looking down at the table, his hands muffling his speech, he said, "We were never engaged."

"What?" the men said in unison.

He sighed and looked up. "It was an act."

Dax popped open a can, sat down, and took a swig. "Well, make it real, then."

"I can't, you idiot."

"How hard can it be, man? Who cares how it started? All you—"

"Do you love her?" Jack interrupted.

"What is this?" he snapped. "An intervention? Are we all going to hold hands and sing 'Kumbaya' when it's over?"

"Do you love her?" Jack repeated calmly.

Marcus balled up his fists to keep from punching something. "It doesn't matter."

"It seems to me it's the only thing that matters." This from Lauren, who had apparently decided to join the touchy-feely ambush.

"It doesn't," he snarled.

"Why the hell not?" Dax said.

"We have work to do," Marcus said, struggling to control his voice. "So if you'll excuse us."

Dax rolled his eyes but got up to follow Jack. "It's your grave, dude." He picked up the five remaining cans of beer. "But you're not getting these."

Rosie could hardly believe she was able to just get up the next morning and act like a normal person. She showered, ate cereal, spackled her puffy, red face with concealer, and took her mother, who had stayed the night at her place, to the train station, all without a whole heart in her chest.

How did people do this? Go through the motions of life with their heart shattered into a million little pieces? As they called her mother's train, Rose started to sniffle. "I'm sorry, Mom." In some ways, the knowledge that she'd disappointed her mother was as bad as the heartbreak. She'd explained the whole stupid story last night, and her mother had held her and stroked her hair, but she couldn't seem to stop apologizing. "I was just so worried about the prospect of you setting me up." She tried to muster a smile. "But you'd probably do a better job than I would."

Her mother's forehead wrinkled in bewilderment. "You want me to set you up?"

"No!" That was the whole point. "But I'm almost thirty!"

"Are you going to turn into a pumpkin on your birthday?" her mom teased.

"No, but you're going to set me up."

"Rose, sweetie. What are you talking about?"

Did her mother not *remember*? "I agreed to let you set me up if I wasn't settled with a guy by the time I was thirty." When her mother continued to look at her blankly, Rosie added, "Two years ago? At Justin's wedding? You talked about it all the time..." She trailed off, furrowing her own brow in confusion. Her mother had talked about it all the time, issuing threats...for a few months. But now that she thought about it, Rosie hadn't actually heard anything about it from her mom for a while now.

Her mom laughed. "Sweetie, I can hardly remember what happened last week, much less two years ago."

Rosie didn't know whether to laugh with her mom or to cry. She'd spent the past year frantically dating, in this race against time, for *nothing*? Well, shit. The universe had thrown so much at her over the past couple weeks, so why not this, too? She hugged her mom. "Well, anyway, I am sorry about this whole mess. I hate that I lied to you."

"You didn't lie, Rose."

"I did, though!" she said, her voice embarrassingly squeaky. "We were deceiving everyone."

"You listen to me," her mother said, shaking a finger in her face. "I saw the two of you together. You didn't lie—not in the way that matters. If you were deceiving anyone, it was yourselves."

Wait. *What?*

"I like him," her mom said, starting to walk away as the line to board the train began moving. Rose stared after her, dumbfounded in addition to heartbroken. "I like his car. Tell him to pick me up next time."

B y seven the next morning, they had a new concept. Marcus wasn't sure if it was better than the one Gail had stolen—he wasn't sure of anything anymore—but it was at least good enough that they could hold their heads up at the noon pitch.

The noon pitch in *Montreal.* "I need to go home and shower and change," said Lauren. "I'll meet you at the airport."

He nodded. He needed to do the same.

They'd spent the night working in Lauren's office, so he stumbled across the hall to his.

"Hey."

He jumped.

"I let myself in. Your assistant wasn't here yet."

"Cary," he said, sighing. He would have to deal with the family fallout, he knew, but he sure as hell wasn't doing it until the pitch was over. "Can we talk about this later?"

"I quit my job."

"*What?*"

"I quit."

"You can't quit." Rosemann Investment Counsel was one of the top private wealth management firms in the country.

"Just because our family started the firm doesn't mean that it can't be run by someone else," he said, answering Marcus's unspoken question.

"But you like the work." He wasn't sure why he was arguing.

"And I'm good at it. But I'll be good at it somewhere else. I'm having lunch with a head hunter today, in fact."

"Why would you do this?"

"Because I'm done working for bullies," he said, looking straight at Marcus.

"Thank you," he whispered, not sure what else to say. The family had always tolerated his father, even after he initiated divorce proceedings against his mother. To hear someone so blatantly standing up and saying, "no," was unprecedented.

Well, not completely unprecedented. Rose had said that very thing to his father last night.

"Rose loves you," said Cary, as if he could hear his thoughts. "Do you love her?"

"I would only end up hurting her."

"That doesn't answer the question."

He looked at his cousin, who was as close as he'd ever had to a sibling. He was amazed at his guts. To just up and quit on his father? He owed Cary the truth. "Yes. I love Rose. But it doesn't matter."

"It would seem like it's the only thing that *does* matter."

It wasn't lost on Marcus that that was exactly what Lauren had said. "I can't hurt her. I can't be like…"

Cary's eyes widened. "Oh, shit. Is that what this is about?" He shook his head. "You're not your father, Marcus."

"How do you know that?" Marcus protested, trying to make Cary understand. "How do *I* know that? I can't risk doing to Rose what my father did to my mother."

Cary smiled. "Well, first of all, I'm pretty sure Rose would never stand for it."

Marcus smiled despite himself. Cary had a point.

"But if you're trying to do the opposite of what your father did, how about, instead of not letting yourself get close to a woman, you pick one and do it right? Love her unconditionally. 'Til death do you part and all that garbage."

Something was happening in Marcus's chest. Something uncomfortable, but powerful. As if forces bigger than he were gathering there.

"Marcus. Look at you. You're miserable and heartbroken. If this is about your mother, think about whether your mother would want that. Would she want you to give up a chance at love?"

A chance at love.

Oh my God. He heard Rose's voice in his head, as clear as if she were standing right beside him.

I love you for real.

Chapter Sixteen

Rosie made it through the day because she turned into a robot. Robot Rosie wrote some thank-you letters to rich people. Robot Rosie went to a meeting and listened to Mr. Carroll talk about nothing.

Robot Rosie even took a call from Leona van der Velde.

"Mr. Carroll isn't in today," she said when Hailey transferred the call, because when the chair of EcoHabitat's board was calling it was always for Mr. Carroll. "But is there something I can help you with?"

"I'm actually calling for you, Rose. I wanted to talk to you about EcoHabitat's website."

That penetrated her robotic fog a bit. "Oh?"

"A few of the board members and I met informally last night and had a look at the new design you did."

"Marcus did it."

"He said you did it together. Regardless, we love it, and we'd like to take it to the full board in January with a recommendation that it be implemented."

Robot Rosie tried to recognize this as a victory, but she was having a hard time mustering the enthusiasm. "Did he also tell you we broke up?" Normally, she wouldn't have spoken so bluntly to Mrs. van der Velde, but robots weren't known for their subtlety.

The older woman was silent for a moment. "He said things were complicated. Although I hope you'll work things out, your personal relationship with Marcus isn't really my concern in this context."

Well, that was a good answer.

"Marcus also said you have a lot of great ideas for EcoHabitat."

Rosie almost laughed. Clearly, guilt-stricken Marcus was trying to throw her a bone after breaking her heart. But whatever, she'd take it. Work was pretty much all she had now. "I try to."

"I'd like to have coffee in the new year and hear about them. I would also appreciate hearing your thoughts on some…staffing challenges."

"That would be great."

As she made her good-byes, Robot Rosie tried to be happy about this development because this was a huge opportunity for EcoHabitat—and for her professionally.

But she couldn't quite manage it.

B y the time the day was almost—blessedly—over, Hailey appeared in Rosie's doorway with her makeup bag.

"Who's tonight's Mr. Thursday Night?"

"Ha!" Rosie meant to laugh, but it came out sounding more like a wail. She'd lost track of the days. It was Thursday. It was the last Thursday before her deadline. The one that didn't matter anymore. The one that never had. "I think I'm going to take a rest until the new year."

Hailey, who did not know about last night's scene, laid a hand on Rosie's arm. She must have sensed that Rosie was struggling. It made her heart wrench. "Want me to do your face anyway?"

"Nah. I'm just going to the Humane Society—I'm going to cut out a little early. I'm thinking of getting a cat."

Hailey cocked her head. "Like, one to keep?"

Rosie tried to smile. "Yeah. One to keep."

While waiting for the elevator in her building and perusing some Humane Society brochures, Rosie's phone dinged.

I know you said you were done internet dating for a while, but you have to check out this guy's profile. He's PERFECT for you. Think about him for when you're back at it in January.

Rosie sighed and clicked on the link in the text from Hailey. It was a profile without a picture. Stepping off the elevator to her floor, she muttered, "Yeah, right." Who put up a dating profile without a picture?

The guy's handle was "Rose Man." Okay, she got it. Cute. And sweet of Hailey to think of her. Hell, maybe she'd even message the guy after the holidays. She scrolled down to look at his profile. Forty, professional in the creative industry, looking for a relationship, blah, blahbity, blah. She skipped to the free text portion as she unlocked her door.

LOOKING FOR A DATE FOR THIS THURSDAY NIGHT. YOU MUST BE: VEGETARIAN, CRUELTY-FREE, LOVER OF BRIGHT COLORS, UNDERAPPRECIATED PROFESSIONALLY, IMPRESSED BY SOLAR POWER. ALSO: BEAUTIFUL, FUNNY, KIND, SEXY AS HELL...AND FORGIVING.

Whaaat? She opened her door to barking.
Barking?
Salt greeted her at the door.

And so did Marcus—Marcus who still had a key to her place from his dog-sitting days.

The sting of humiliation, as strong as it had been the night before, prevented her from throwing herself into his arms. "What are you—"

He held up a hand. "No talking."

She was instantly transported back to that night he'd stayed over when she was drunk, and the spectacular "no talking" sex they'd had the next morning. Not talking was easier when you were in the middle of shagging the world's hottest CEO. It was harder when you felt like your heart was going to explode out of your chest thanks to a perfect storm of confusion, heartbreak, and longing.

Grabbing her hand, he led her down the hallway to her bedroom. She followed, but tugged her hand out of his grasp.

The first thing she noticed was the lack of a bed. Okay, no, it was there—it had just been pushed against the far wall next to a...ladder?

She looked up. "Actions speak louder than words," she read, and then she clamped her hand over her mouth, belatedly remembering she wasn't supposed to talk.

He had finished the stenciling. Her poor, poor heart. It did a great leap then, springing up on a tiny trampoline made of hope and love and probably a little bit of lust, too. Screw this no talking thing. "Did you put Hailey up to calling me just now? Are you Rose Man?" she whispered, hardly even able to look at him.

"I am. I want to be."

An involuntary wail ripped from her throat. She couldn't help it. She'd been trying to play it cool—hadn't she *finally* learned to protect herself? But then Salt, who had followed them into the bedroom, barked.

"Sit!" Marcus snapped, and Salt sat.

"You didn't give her back," Rose said.

"I didn't give her back. I didn't do a lot of other things, either. I didn't pitch on Magnifique."

Rose narrowed her eyes, trying to make sense of the puzzle pieces he was dangling in front of her. "You let Gail win?"

"I let Gail win."

"Why?"

He grinned. "Magnifique tests on animals." Then he shrugged. "And it just wasn't worth it. It was one account. It wasn't a referendum on the worth of my company or my value as a human being. I see that now. If my father doesn't approve of me now, he never will."

Well, no matter how much Marcus had hurt her, that was a sentiment she could get behind.

He cleared his throat, then swallowed hard. "I also

didn't see that I'm not him. That I'm not doomed to repeat his mistakes."

She furrowed her brow, confused, feeling like there was nothing to hold onto in the midst of a storm that was hitting her suddenly.

"I love you, Rose. And if I don't let myself love you, my father wins. But I don't even care about that. He can have the last word. The important thing is that if I don't let myself love you, *I* lose. I lose *everything*."

"I thought you said you *couldn't* love."

"I thought so. I'd told myself a story about myself, see. It was…" He trailed off, his fist clenching as if angry. At himself? "Easier that way. But then…you."

"But I'm so…" Rosie trailed off. She'd been going to say *wrong. Unsuitable. Common.*

"Perfect?" he supplied, finishing her sentence.

She thought of Jo's refrain. *If you want something good, you have to take a risk.*

"I'm getting a cat," she said quickly, before she could talk herself out of it, let her pride get the better of her.

It was his turn to furrow his brow. "Uh, okay."

Crap. That had been less of a non-sequitur in her head. "I'm getting a cat because I want something to stick," she tried to explain. "All those dates I went on, all those animals I boarded—nothing ever stuck."

"You were afraid of getting hurt again," he said. Because he knew her. "You've been hurt a lot."

"Yes." Her eyes filled.

"I'm sorry," he said. "All this time, I was trying *not* to break your heart. Not to be like my father. But I did just the same. It was the last thing I wanted."

She wanted to say that it wasn't the same. That even if he had made a misstep—even if he didn't, couldn't, wouldn't love her—he would never be his father. He was too good a man for that. But everything was so muddled in her head, all she could come out with was, "I want you to stick."

He made a sharp choking noise before clearing his throat and smiling at her. "This cat of yours is going to have to get along with Salt."

"How did you even get Salt in the building?" It was easier to just ask a mundane question. Her heart needed a break.

"I disguised her as a Chihuahua." When she swatted him, he smiled. "I just walked her up here. No one gave me any trouble."

That figured. "Why does the world just bend to your will? I get that you're a big fancy CEO dude, but—"

And then he was kissing her—interrupting her speech with his mouth on hers. Just like the first time. It wasn't as gentle as that time, though. His lips moved against hers with confidence, as if he knew that when his tongue tested the seam of her mouth, she would open for him. And she did. But then, just as suddenly, he pulled back. "Rose," he rasped, dragging his lips along her throat.

"Hmmm?"

"Stop talking."

Epilogue

Six months later

"Our final item of business is the executive director's report," said Leona. Marcus admired the way Leona ran a meeting—she kept things moving along, which was something he appreciated in general.

But also in this specific instance. Because he had shit to do tonight.

If Rose and Leona hadn't ganged up on him and guilted him into taking up his mother's seat on the EcoHabitat board, he could be doing those things right now.

Well, actually, that wasn't true.

Because he needed EcoHabitat's new executive director to do them.

He tried to pay attention as Rose ran through a presentation updating them on projects and showed some slides on the finances for the final stage of office renovations. It was hard, though, because as she stood there in her conservative "presenting to the board" outfit," which was a gray blouse and blood red pencil skirt that fit her like a second skin, his mind kept sliding back to what she had done to him this morning in his bed—and forward to what he planned to do right back to her tonight.

"Thank you, Rose," said Leona. "I know I speak for the full board when I say how pleased we are with this detailed update." She smiled. "And to have you with us in your new capacity."

Rose opened her mouth to say something, but Leona just kept going. "I need a motion to adjourn."

His hand shot up.

"Marcus!" Rosie protested, when her boyfriend started physically towing her toward the door. "I should really stay and chat with some of the board members!" She didn't protest too much, though. In truth, she was exhausted. Even though the board had already demonstrated its confidence in her by approving some of the projects she told Leona about months ago—and, of course, by sending Mr. Carroll packing and naming her to replace him— she'd been crazy-nervous about her first meeting as executive director. Time for a soak in Marcus's giant bath. Or her tiny bath. Didn't matter which house they ended up at. She just wanted to chill out.

"Where are we going?" she asked, when she realized that Marcus, who had, uncharacteristically, driven his own car to the meeting, was getting on the Gardiner Expressway.

"I have a new billboard up I want to show you."

"Ah, Crazy Bert!" she said. She loved that Marcus and Lauren had kept Crazy Bert even though the firm had landed a bunch of new upscale clients in recent months.

He pulled over into the right lane and slowed down. "It's coming up. Open your window so you can get a really good look."

A weird request, but she obeyed, leaning out and shielding her eyes against the setting summer sun.

"I think it's my best ad yet," Marcus said.

"I can't wait to—oh!"

Oh.

The billboard in question was painted bright pink. And in giant, sparkly silver letters it said, "Rose Verma, will you marry me? Love, Marcus Rosemann."

She started shaking then, and laughing, and crying—everything at once.

"Open the glove compartment."

"Marcus."

"Don't talk. Just do it."

She smiled at the now-familiar directive—it had become a central feature of their sex life—and forced her clumsy hands to do what he said. She knew what she would find there.

She opened the small box to reveal his mother's ring. The ring she'd given back to him that night he'd finished the stenciling in her bedroom.

"So we had our happily-ever-after moment six months ago," he said, pulling off the highway. "And I thought then that you are probably the only woman in the world who would mark a happily-ever-after by *giving back* an engagement ring."

She laughed, almost unable to look at him, his profile so dear to her as he maneuvered the car to a side street, parked, and cut the engine.

When he turned to face her full on, his gray-blue eyes filmed with liquid, it was too much, and she had to bury her head in her hands. "Your mother's ring," she said.

"No," he said, his voice sharp. "Your ring." Then he gentled his tone as he took the box from her. "It's been your ring from the moment I met you." Popping open the box, he held it out to her. "What do you say? Salt and I want you and Pepper to move in." When she just shook her head, unable to make her mouth form the single word she was screaming inside her head, he added, "Or we can live at your place. But you'll have to run for the condo board and get the breed ban overturned."

She held out her hand, quivering as he slid the ring on her finger. "Nah," she croaked. "Pepper likes your place." She grinned. "So the answer is yes."

He heaved a shaky sigh and started the car again. "Well, damn, that's a relief."

"Marcus Rosemann! Were you nervous? Did you really think I'd say anything other than yes?"

"I was pretty sure when you got a white cat and named it Pepper that I was in the clear. Still, a man gets nervous when his entire life is on the line. Especially when he's just publicly declared himself on a pink billboard. It's not as easy as you think to—"

"Marcus," she interrupted.

"Yeah?"

"Let's not talk for a while."

Shooting her a wolfish grin, he unbuckled his seat belt, leaned over and kissed her—a slow, deep, possessive kiss that was, even after all these months, like a drug. There was just enough space left in her consciousness for a rogue thought to float to the surface.

"Oh my God," she wailed, pushing him away.

"I thought we were not talking," he said, looking adorably bewildered. "What's wrong?"

"My name really *is* going to be Rose Rosemann now."

Acknowledgments

Tracy Montoya has always been a super talented editor, but I feel like with this book in particular, she picked up a manuscript that was, well...a little bit of a hot mess and shook it really hard until the book it was always meant to be fell out. I'm not really sure how you do that, Tracy, but I'm so thankful that you do!

Courtney Miller-Callihan, superagent and friend, I am so lucky that we are a team. Thank you for your relentless and cheerful advocacy—and for sending David Bowie paper dolls. Never let it be said that yours is not a full-service agency.

The usual suspects Audra North, Sandra Owens, and Erika Olbricht can never be thanked enough for the many aspects of their awesomeness. In addition to helping me tackle this book (see above: hot mess), they apparently never tire of receiving repetitive, neurotic emails. Thank you for making my whole life, not to mention my books, better.

Finally, thanks are due to friends JB and Pete Breton for straightening me out on a lot of the details related to advertising agency life. I miss you guys. Rosé on the virtual stoop soon? (What is FaceTime for, if not stoop drinking?)

About the Author

Jenny Holiday started writing at age nine when her fourth-grade teacher gave her a notebook and told her to start writing stories. That first batch featured mass murderers on the loose, alien invasions, and hauntings. From then on, she was always writing, often in her diary, where she liked to decorate declarations of existential angst with nail polish teardrops. Later, she channeled her penchant for scribbling into a more useful format, picking up a PhD in geography and then working in PR. Eventually, she figured out that happy endings were more fun than alien invasions. You can follow her on Twitter at @jennyholi or visit her on the web at jennyholiday.com.

Discover the **49th Floor** *series...*

Also by Jenny Holiday